# LIGHT

# *Torgny Lindgren*

# LIGHT

Translated from the Swedish
by Tom Geddes

HARVILL
*An Imprint of* HarperCollins*Publishers*

First published in Sweden in 1987
under the title *Ljuset* by Norstedts Förlag, Stockholm

First published in Great Britain in 1992
by Harvill
an imprint of HarperCollins*Publishers*,
77/85 Fulham Palace Road,
Hammersmith, London W6 8JB

9 8 7 6 5 4 3 2 1

A CIP catalogue record for this book
is available from the British Library.

The Publishers gratefully acknowledge the
financial support of the Swedish Institute
towards the publication of this book in
English.

ISBN 0-00-271171-0

Photoset in Linotron Ehrhardt by
Rowland Phototypesetting Ltd,
Bury St Edmunds, Suffolk
Printed and bound in Great Britain by
Hartnolls Limited, Bodmin, Cornwall

. . . and the Servant of the King did cause
the Pig that was a Dragon to be hanged,
and did cause its Master to be punished
likewise in great Ignominy, and
great was the Unrest. Let him save
himself who can.

SAYINGS OF CHADIUS, FOL. I

*Where rabbits abound, nothing remains as it was.*

It was late autumn when Jasper brought the Sickness to Kadis. He had been to Nordingrå to find himself a woman but had not found one. He knew she would have close-set eyes. And her nose would be narrow and high-bridged and she would be slightly knock-kneed and have a birthmark on her right cheek and a little gap between her front teeth, and whatever she might have been christened, he would call her Maria.

He searched for three days and he described her in detail to everyone he met, but no one would admit that she existed.

Then his food ran out. He had had barley bread and blood pudding and raw turnips in a birch-bark basket on his back. He did not want to beg: if the woman he was looking for had existed she would have despised him if she had heard that he was begging for his bread. So he went back the same way he had come.

He slept under a fir tree at the foot of a mountain that did not yet have a name. He cried himself to sleep. He wept for the woman who did not exist, just as if she had been dead instead of non-existent.

All his life he had been convinced that she existed; he had believed in her as he had believed in God.

So then he bought a pregnant rabbit – that was in Umeå – a big rabbit with black tufts on its ears and a cross of grey specks on its back. He did not want to come home completely empty-handed. He paid with a copper buckle that Yvar, the smith in Kadis, had made for him. And he made a bed of grass for her in his basket and fed her with nettle leaves.

9

When he got back home to Kadis he went to the water gully in front of the chapel. He had promised to show the woman to everyone who wanted to see her. And the other unmarried men and even the children turned up at once.

"She doesn't exist in Nordingrå," he said. "She's never existed."

"So she was just a fiction that you invented," said one of the unmarried men.

"She existed for me," said Jasper. "And she lived in Nordingrå."

"Nothing can be like that. To exist for one person but not for anyone else."

"No one can really tell the difference between existing and not existing," said Jasper. "And she used to come to me at night."

"You made a whore of the fiction," the man went on. "You called it to you in your sleep to make a whore of it. You were in a sort of trance, both you and the woman you invented."

"The soles of my feet are bleeding," said Jasper. "Would I have gone all the way to Nordingrå for a fiction?"

And someone said: "You'll have to find yourself another one."

"There is no other one for me," said Jasper.

And one of the little boys said: "When I grow up I'll go to Nordingrå and find her."

But Könik the carpenter, who had been unmarried till recently but now had a wife called Eira, said: "That's not right."

"What isn't right?" said Jasper.

"The woman," said Könik. "You inventing her. And her not existing."

His hair and beard were brownish-black and he was fairly heavily built and he had a furrow in his brow that went a bit deeper and darker when he said that it wasn't right.

And he continued: "If she had existed, if you had found her in Nordingrå, then you would have had to invent another woman for yourself straight away. Instead of the woman that existed. Things will never be exactly right."


What had they been doing in Kadis that day? All the people.

They had been to Mass, because it was the day of rest.

They had rested after the midday meal, all the hundreds of them that there were; even the children had had to lie down and pretend to sleep for a while.

The women had gone to collect the animals as they came out of the forest. Ten cows had been missing and they'd had to search for them on the common, because there were mushrooms everywhere now, especially the sort called cow-mushrooms.

They had milked all the cows.

The men had met and decided that the cattle should go out again for another ten days. They had decided that it would be winter after that.

They had eaten whitefish and sea-fowl.

They had listened to the priest, who had spoken of the incomprehensible size and fullness of the universe and said that everything is made in wisdom and the earth abounds in laws of nature and of property. Grass grows for the cattle and corn for the people so that they can farm their land till eventide. Peace and order flow from the earth and pour over us like rain.

And they had said: Amen.


And now several of them began to leave. Dusk was falling and it was getting cold.

"But in my basket," said Jasper, "in my basket I've got something that's sure and true."

They came back at that, the ones who had started to leave.

And as he took out the peg and undid the clasp to open the lid, he said:

"I paid three silver coins for her."

And:

"She was covered by a hare on Saint Michael's Day and the hare was as big as a kid ready for slaughter."

But just as he was lifting the rabbit out of the basket, a flea jumped out of her fur and bit him on the little finger of his left hand, by the cuticle – and that little flea was the Great Sickness.

"That's odd," he said, "animal fleas don't usually bite people."

But he nipped it and crushed it between his thumb and fore-finger.

They looked at her, the rabbit – she was fat and clearly preg-nant, she swelled out in all directions, and it was impossible to see what she really looked like, her ordinary shape was lost in the fat and excess.

And Jasper explained the essential nature of rabbits:

"Man can never comprehend the rabbit – no, not even if we live to be a thousand can we solve the riddle of the rabbit.

"Their fur is soft and warm, it's like the hair in a woman's armpit. Stroking a rabbit is like dipping your hand in warm milk straight from the cow. And the flesh is as soft and white as butter. You're full for a whole week when you've eaten rabbit, even the cooked meat seems to have offspring and multiply itself.

"Man may be made in the image of God, but there is also a God Who created the rabbit in His own image, a God of liveli-ness and quivering and fear and fecundity.

"The female rabbit can have ten litters a year. And ten young'uns every time. Who can reckon up how incredibly many rabbits there would be in the end? Uncountable, that's what rabbits try to be. The female rabbit has so much love that she can never be still, she never stops running about, and some part of her body is always twitching.

"Yes, the rabbit is a creator.

"And rabbits can hear everything, they can sit in front of a clover bud and hear it sprouting and wait for the petals to come.

"And rabbits can die of almost anything, a gust of wind, a rain-drop, a flea-bite, a hailstone."

And one of the boys asked him: "Does she have a name?"

"She's called Maria."

"Can a rabbit really be called Maria?"

"She has a finer name than any other because she's the first rabbit in this part of the country.

"And what you should know is that where rabbits abound, nothing remains as it was, miracles happen, and nothing is sure and certain, and there's no point in talking about what's right or wrong or possible or impossible."

That was what he said to Könik.

He had a strange way of talking, had Jasper. He always seemed to drone on, he never stopped, and now it sounded just as if he was going to start on some absurd and foolish story, and God knows what would be in it – evil and sudden death, and strangers with gold bands around their heads, and fathers who coupled with their daughters, and fantastic beasts, and child-stealing, and royal messengers who made a fool of God and the whole world, and dragons and their masters who were hanged by the rope.

No one could be bothered to listen to him for long.

Occasionally someone would ask him: "Why are you telling me this story?"

"Stories," Jasper would always say, "are probably just told to give people a sense of wonder."


In the evening, Yvar the smith came to see Jasper. Jasper still lived in his parents' house, which was behind the open space they called the market-place.

"I've heard that you've exchanged silver for a rabbit," he said. "I thought it was only Avar who had silver here in Kadis."

"She's pregnant," said Jasper. "A hare as big as a boar has put at least fifteen young'uns in her."

"Have you got any more silver?" said Yvar. "Silver isn't for exchanging for rabbits."

"That was all I had," said Jasper.

But then Jasper's father said:

"He went to fetch a woman who didn't exist. And he bought a rabbit with silver he didn't have. And the rabbit will soon be covered by the devil himself if he goes on like this."

Then Jasper suddenly had to rush out of the door and vomit. And Yvar went home.

Jasper vomited till he was empty, then he lay down on the straw inside the door. The fever in his body broke out almost straight away. He began to shake with cold and sweated so much that the straw around him became soaked and began to smell of mould. He vomited twice again at dawn, this time just blood, and then he died.

When Jasper's father carried him out to the woodpile he saw that the dead man's face was covered in dark red sores.

Then his father went to Yvar – and it was still early in the morning – carrying the rabbit, in his son's basket, on his back.

"I'd like you to make a jaw-lock for Jasper," he said. "He's lying on the woodpile. So that he can't open his mouth through-out all eternity."

That's how it was in Kadis: what was right and proper was more important and of greater value than anything else.

And he was weeping and snuffling so heart-rendingly that he had to repeat jaw-lock three times before Yvar understood it.

Then from Könik the carpenter he ordered a coffin for his son and a hutch for the rabbit, a little box made of rough fir-branches. That rabbit hutch was the last object that Könik made to serve life for a time that was going to be so long that he would afterwards have neither words nor name to describe the length of it.

Except for a swinging chair for a child whose conception and birth would soon occur in such a manner that Könik would rather have made it a coffin than a chair.

14

Yvar worked all day long on the jaw-lock, using metal that he himself had hammered and rivets he had forged and copper wire he had made. He worked at a little anvil he had brought with him to the woodpile, and by evening Jasper's mouth was so bound up and forged together that it would never open again. It was a jaw-lock more durable than the jaw itself. But by then Yvar was so weak and feeble that his hands would no longer obey him and there were black spots and flames of fire dancing before his eyes. Jasper's father had to support him and put his arms round his chest and carry him home.

Yvar lay in the dark and could feel with his fingers great pustules breaking out all over his body. They were growing even as he felt them with his fingertips, and before it was light he was dead.

So both Jasper and Yvar were carried to Könik for coffins. They were laid out in the little oblong house next to the dried timber, and everyone in Kadis came to look at them.

The priest came too. He anointed their eyes and noses and ears and hands and feet and mouths – yes, he even managed to push his thin forefinger in through Jasper's jaw-lock and touch his pouting lips. The people standing nearest could see the priest shaking so much that the oil splashed out of the little clay bottle, and many of them thus got splashes of the last anointing oil on themselves. These were the last little drops of the sacrament that were administered in Kadis for a fearfully long time.

The priest had been in Kadis for several years. It was the Bishop who had sent him north, not to any one place but to nowhere in particular. People had been moving north for a long time, villages were growing up in those desolate lands, perhaps even towns, and someone had to go to them with all that was holy and necessary.

He was dreadfully thin, despite eating enough for three men. When Könik married, they had counted the pieces of bread and the grouse and ptarmigan and the portions of meat and salmon, and all the time he took three where others took one, and Jasper had said that that's how it had to be, he had to eat for the entire Trinity. Nevertheless he remained the thinnest and boniest man in Kadis. His nose was long and sharp, like an axe-blade; his bones showed through his robe like hewn-off branches, and the skin on his hands hung loose and slack. But his eyes were large and filled with wonder; they looked almost liquid amidst the general aridity of the rest.

He had been in all the countries anyone had ever heard of, bishops had sent him here and there and everywhere, and he had gathered secrets and knowledge the way squirrels gather fir cones.

He knew almost everything, and therefore wanted to know no more. He didn't want to know the name of the place to which he had come; that's what he said to them: "Don't tell me the name of your village or town or whatever sort of place you think this is, just build me a chapel and let me be."

So they built the chapel for him, and Könik made a gigantic cross from a topped fir tree. Out of fairness they didn't ask his name, they just called him the priest – they responded to namelessness with namelessness and no one ever said Kadis to him.

He was the first priest they had had. They were grateful that he attended to everything that was holy and necessary for them, but they all thought that he seemed in a permanent state of despair: wherever he went he was constantly wringing his hands. His bony fingers were bent and twisted in every joint, and they must have got like that because he had wrung his hands incessantly all his life.

Now he stood there in all his wisdom looking at Jasper and Yvar whom he had just anointed, and he recognized the Sickness that had killed them. And he wrung and twisted his hands so that it seemed they would never come apart again. He had had the Great Sickness described to him on innumerable occasions,

16

he knew all there was to know about it. Up to now he and the Sickness had always travelled separate paths, he had always managed to be sent away from it, in fact he had come to believe that he and it would never meet.

Or that the Great Sickness existed only in the knowledge thereof.

But now he saw it face to face.

He began to shake and tremble like a wizened fir tree in a storm. The tremors started in his ankles and moved upwards to his knees and spread to his hips and chest and shoulders.

And his heart began to thump so loud in his bony chest that it sounded like the tapping of a woodpecker on a hollow trunk – everyone could hear it. Nothing like it had ever been heard in Kadis before.

But he did nothing. Then eventually he said: "What is this place called?"

"Kadis."

And someone asked: "What is your name?"

And he answered: "Blasius."

Then someone said:

"So at last we've introduced ourselves."

Then all they could see was that he was moving his lips. He was no longer able to make himself heard above the noise from within his breast. And finally his heart fell silent. He was the third to die. He died of plague and knowledge.

The next day Könik's father died, the man who'd lost his hand in a wolf trap he'd made himself. And Jasper's father. And Yvar's wife and one of his children.

And several others.

"It's not right," said Könik. "Death has lost its senses and its sight and is flailing around blindly."

On the last day he was alive Jasper's father had brought out the rabbit hutch and before he died he saw that the rabbit had given birth to seven young ones. And the last thing he said was: "Who'll look after the rabbits now?"

17

When ten people had died, Könik dragged up a phrase from a deep cleft in his memory, something he had once heard but had completely forgotten.

"I wonder if it can be the Great Sickness."

It was in the evening when he said it; the light coming through the two apertures by the door was hardly enough for them to see each other, he and his wife Eira. He had been planing wood for coffins all day long and he was tired. But he could see Eira turn so pale that her cheeks began to shine in the darkness.

Eira was unusually, even extraordinarily, short. If Könik had taken the trouble to think long and hard enough he might have found the word "dwarf" buried in his memory, but he contented himself with the words "My Little One". Her smallness was just enough for his love to develop with only a slight twinge of pain. Her size was more or less acceptable – if her body had been a little bit smaller and her head any bigger he would have come to pity her and perhaps even despise her.

Now she rose from the stool she was sitting on and pulled her skirt over her head and crept down between the sheepskin covers. Könik couldn't bring himself to say anything except: "Yes, My Little One, the Great Sickness, Little One."

And she didn't get up the next morning. It was as if she thought: "This isn't a real day, I'm not going to bother with it."

Nor did she get up the following day. She lay there completely still. The only parts of her that moved at all were her eyelids.

No, she didn't get up any more.

Könik gave her warm milk – he had to take care of the milking now – and he cooked barley porridge for her, he fed her and he lifted her in and out of bed when necessary. When darkness fell and put a stop to his coffin-making he sat by her and carved off thin strips from a smoked side of lamb and put them in her mouth.

He felt her forehead at frequent intervals to see whether she had a fever, and he put his hands under the covers and stroked her breasts and stomach and thighs to see whether any pustules

18

had begun to break out. But she answered when he spoke to her. Her voice had always been faint and slight, and now in her paralysis it had faded even more.

"Are you in pain?"

"No."

"Would you like honey in your warm milk?"

"Yes."

"Do you ache in your armpits?"

"No."

"Shall I tell you what a strange cloud I saw over the river today?"

"Yes."

"Can I hold you in my arms for a while in front of the fire?"

"Yes."

And every evening he told her who had just been brought to him and laid out in his workshop, and who were now lying there waiting. Or how he would say:

"It isn't right."

He brought two young rabbits in for her too, for her to have in the bed with her.

There was no one now who owned Jasper's rabbits.

But Könik couldn't bring himself to lie beside her; he lay in the corner, by the woodbox.

It wouldn't have been right.

One evening he just sat there, trying to see her.

"Birds," he said to her, "birds lie down with their legs in the air, they protect themselves by pretending to be dead. When they hear the hunter."

"Yes," said Eira.

"They think they're going to save themselves, they think salvation must consist of some sort of deception."

"Yes."

"Are you a bird?" said Könik.

"Yes," she said. "I might be."

And then they fell silent.

"We've got to stay close to one another anyway," he said. "Close," he said, "that means what you can enclose in your arms, that's all the word means."

Then he groped his way over to his corner and crept down into the bed.

But a few moments later he cried out to her at the top of his voice: "It's not right!"

"Birds can do it."

"But man must stand upright while he still can."

Eira didn't know that he possessed such a voice, she had never heard it before, and although she was in a state of near paralysis, her whole body began to quiver, and she trembled herself to sleep.

The burial ground was outside the village wall.

The wall wasn't a real wall but a fence made of lopped and stripped young fir trees. Their forefathers had called it the wall; they wanted to have a wall round Kadis.

Sometimes Könik went out there early in the morning, carrying a bundle of stakes and a knife. He was putting markers on the graves so that people would know who was lying where. He carved signs on the stakes with his knife, signs that meant a name or a trade or a deformity or something else that could be understood or interpreted.

To make everything right. The right person, right grave, right stake, the right signs on the stakes.

Now all the rabbits were being taken care of by those who happened to be still alive in Kadis. Some of the rabbits had just been set free to look after themselves. Könik put the empty rabbit hutch as a marker on Jasper's grave.

Könik wanted to make coffins that it would be easy to rise from. So he used the thinnest wood for the lids and fastened them with two pegs that could simply be knocked off from beneath. He didn't put any pegs at all on the children's coffins, but just laid the lids on as covers – he didn't want to frighten them unnecessarily.

The wood that he'd already dried was only enough for a little while, and he soon had to split and use such newly-felled timber that the wood he was now planing felt like dough. The men were dying first, and they needed bigger coffins; the women and children managed to keep going longer. When the men died, there were usually women and children left to mourn them, but when later the women and children had to be buried, there were only a few neighbours and distant relations left. The simple fact was that the more that died, the fewer there were to mourn them.

Death still remained fundamentally just as wretched and depressing as ever, the physical pain and the mental torment were the same, but there was nothing remarkable about it any more – it was just like the rabbits, the young rabbits were nowhere near so unusual as the old doe rabbit had been at the beginning.

And she had been killed now, the rabbit called Maria.

Jasper had had a half-brother, his name was Önde and he lived by the village wall just behind the chapel. He'd had a woman called Cecilia, but she had deserted him. A fur trader had come up from the south one day, a giant of a man with red hair, carrying the skins in bales on his back. When he disappeared he took Cecilia with him. She carried the squirrel skins.

Afterwards Önde had a beard comb that he hadn't had before, a comb that combed out lice, it might even have been a silver one. Perhaps he had sold Cecilia.

Everything about Önde was uncertain.

It was Önde who had killed and eaten the old doe rabbit. He made a hat out of the skin, a furry conical cap.

He had a cow. It was probably the cow that kept him alive. He had two pieces of land and used to rake up leaves on the common further up the river. There was no order in his life. Now he sometimes felled timber for Könik. But not every day and when Könik asked him to: only when he felt like it.

If ever strangers came to Kadis – and that did actually happen from time to time because the only path up the river led to Kadis – they would always be sent to Önde. Önde may have been regarded as a good-for-nothing, but he was never at a loss for an answer.

"We don't know anything," they would say. "But go to Önde."


Könik had a staff on which he cut a notch for every coffin he finished. It hung on a peg on the wall in front of him. One day he noticed it was completely covered in notches, there was no room for even one more little scratch, and when he saw that, when he saw the mass of notches and suddenly realized how many dead people there were numbered and represented on the staff, he was filled with an incomprehensible cheerfulness.

It was about midday and he had just fed Eira. She was still lying as if paralyzed.

And he began to laugh, he laughed for safety's sake and to liberate himself, it was a laugh that was inordinately bigger than himself, a roar of laughter that healed him for the moment.

No one could hear him, and he didn't want to live with such cheerfulness pent up inside him in such adverse times.

And a refreshing certainty came over him like a bright light: that he was trapped in a great fiction that someone had just thought up, that it was in a story that he was hammering and planing and striving to give a comprehensible, physical shape to death, perhaps the story that Jasper had begun with the rabbit, a story that would end by his smashing it to pieces and stepping out of it.

So death really had come to be no longer simply tragic, but also laughable; it was the very numbers of deaths that were so killingly funny.

He was laughing and planing in slow, steady movements. Then a shadow fell on him and he raised his eyes to see a stranger standing in the doorway.

"I heard you in here," said the man, and Könik noticed immediately from his accent that he was from the east, from over the other side of the sea.

"It's the plane," said Könik. "It's squealing because the wood is so new."

"Is this place called Kadis?"

"Yes, this is Kadis."

"It seems quiet and peaceful here in Kadis."

"We're all getting on with our own affairs," said Könik. "We're a quiet and serious people."

"There are lots of houses," the man said. "But I don't see any people."

He had a leather bag hanging over his chest. It wasn't big, but it looked heavy.

"A lot of them have lain down to rest for a while," said Könik. "But they'll be up again."

The man said his name was Olavus and that he traded in all kinds of wares.

"There's supposed to be a poison that heals people who are paralyzed," said Könik. He had never heard of any such poison.

23

"I haven't got any goods with me," said Olavus the trader. "I want to buy, not sell."

Then he added: "You're planing boards for a coffin."

"There's a need for everything," said Könik. "Even coffins."

"Who has died?" asked Olavus suspiciously.

"No one in particular. And someone has to die some time."

And though it was not to the point, he said: "My wife is lying in bed and can't walk."

"So if I want to buy, or if I want to know whether something is for sale, or if I want to know what there is in Kadis," said Olavus, "then it's you I should talk to."

"I don't know anything," said Könik. "But go and see Önde."

Könik had put the plane down to show that he was happy to talk for a while longer. He was wondering about the leather bag that this man Olavus had hanging over his chest.

"Where can I find Önde?" Olavus asked.

"He lives up by the wall just behind the chapel."

"I didn't see any wall as I came," said Olavus.

"No, there isn't a wall, but that's what it's called."

"So his name's Önde, then."

"Yes. Önde."

Könik brushed off the wood-shavings that were sticking to his tunic. "I can go a bit of the way with you," he said.

When they got to the chapel he pointed to Önde's house. There was smoke coming out of the opening in the roof, he was at home.

"I've also heard," said Könik, "that there are blades that are so sharp that they cut branches like butter."

"Yes," said Olavus.

"It would have been good if you'd had your wares with you. If you'd had a blade like that."

He stood and watched the trader go in through Önde's door. He wouldn't leave Önde's empty-handed – or at least he wouldn't be aware that he was empty-handed.

*

24

They sat down on the wooden benches by the fire, Önde and Olavus. Önde stoked up the fire and Olavus said who he was. And Önde went out and fetched a keg from the earthen cellar and offered him something he called beer. He took down two wooden cups from the wall. Beer – well, it might have been beer, or could have been beer if it had had some sweetness in it so that it could have fermented and not just turned sour.

"I haven't drunk a beer like this for a long time," said Olavus. "Not since I visited the Bishop two years ago."

"I brew it myself," said Önde.

"Sharp but not bitter. And a fresh and stimulating smell."

"That's the birch sap," said Önde.

"Have many people died here in Kadis lately?" asked Olavus.

"Are we still talking about the beer?" said Önde.

"No. Now we're talking about death."

"My grandfather died three years ago," said Önde. "He got the split branch of a fir tree through his stomach when he was felling trees. The water ran out of him in such quantities that he shrivelled up and died."

Önde's grandfather had died a few days before, covered in pustules and with great speed.

"Oh," said Olavus.

"He was gone seventy," said Önde, "but it was as clear and golden as birth waters."

"And nobody else?" Olavus asked. "No others?"

"Not that I can think of right now," Önde replied.

Olavus forced down a few sips of the beer.

"There's something that's called the Great Sickness," he said.

And Önde repeated it slowly and solemnly, that was something he perhaps ought to learn and memorize: the Great Sickness.

"And why is that particular sickness called great? Isn't all fatal sickness just as great?"

"It's inordinately greater than we human beings," said

25

Olavus, "that's why it's called great. Man is a little flea compared with the Great Sickness."

And he demonstrated with his right hand what happens to man the little flea: he nipped and crushed it between his thumb and forefinger.

"What is the nature of this illness?" Önde asked. "The Great Sickness."

"It's fever and vomiting and blood and red pustules and black pustules."

"So you've seen it?"

"I've kept to the furthermost extremities of the world just so that I never have to see it."

And it was strange how he gave a little sob when he spoke of the furthermost extremities of the world.

But, he explained – and he lowered his voice so that Önde had to lean forward towards him to hear what he said – he had been collecting information about it, he had found out all there was to know about the Great Sickness. It had been his special illness for a long time now: he had committed to memory everything that could be said about the Great Sickness. And at last he knew that there was just one cure, one single remedy that could save the world, and that was why he had come to Kadis.

"I see," said Önde. "Well, of course. But what might it be? This remedy."

"The musk gland of the beaver," Olavus replied. "It's the musk gland of the beaver."

They sat in silence for a while thinking about this insignificant little thing, that little lump in the beaver's groin, that small and withered yet incredibly potent little pea.

"You don't mention God," said Onde. "God can't save the world, then?"

Önde's cow stood tied to the wall just opposite the door. She sighed gloomily from time to time as she stood over her trough of dried leaves.

"God has been tried in every way and everywhere," said

Olavus. "God as bread, and people have drunk Him, and made Him into powder to mix with porridge, and they have spread Him on the pustules. But nothing has come of it."

"Well," said Önde, "as far as God is concerned we just have to keep on trying."

"Now the learned men are saying that God Himself resides in the Great Sickness," said Olavus. "And God can't be driven out by God."

"But has anyone thought of trying the devil?" Önde suggested.

He wanted to let it be known that there was knowledge even in Kadis.

"Certainly. People have tried pestle and mortar on the devil and dissolved him in water and baked him in cakes. But he's powerless. He tastes bitter but he's powerless."

"If the Great Sickness came here to Kadis," said Önde, "we'd let it be. We wouldn't disturb it unnecessarily. We never molest any stranger who comes here."

A little rabbit appeared from somewhere, perhaps from the trough of leaves. Önde lifted it up on to his lap.

So now they knew for certain that beavers' musk glands would do it. In foreign lands there had been cases of people already dead beginning to breathe again when given beavers' musk glands.

And Olavus instructed Önde:

The beaver had no knowledge of good or evil, he was unacquainted with either God or the devil, he was the cleanest and the dirtiest of all the animals, he did not even distinguish between land and water. And right in the hindquarters of the beaver, in the most unconscious part of the beaver's body, between the opening of the gut and the sexual organ, there in the darkness between life and death, unmoving yet in constant motion, alive and yet dead, the musk gland lay hidden.

That was what the secret was. That was what its power came from.

So he, Olavus, had been exchanging goods in the remotest parts of the world, especially in the northernmost reaches, always bigger for smaller, constantly striving for the tiniest and most easily carried: silver and gold.

That was what he had in his bag.

Now all that remained was to exchange the silver and gold for beavers' musk glands.

A bag of beavers' musk glands, and life and all the riches of the earth would be his.

One thing he knew: Of all the rarities of Creation the musk gland of the beaver was the most exceptional. He had looked for it in vain for more than a year, and sometimes he had said to himself in desperation: There is no such thing as beaver's musk gland, beaver's musk gland is just a word and an illusion.

But now people in Umeå had said: Perhaps in Kadis.

"Yes, yes," said Önde.

The cow sighed, and from beyond the house not a sound could be heard, they had heard nothing since they sat down by the hearth. It was very quiet in Kadis.

"It's very quiet here in Kadis," Olavus said.

"Yes," said Önde.

"And peaceful, and somehow empty of people."

"Yes."

"I've wondered a lot," said Olavus the trader, "I've wondered a lot since arriving here where all the people are."

"They're in the forest," Önde replied, "a long way up the river, right up by the mountains, by the streams and tributaries. This is the time of year when we trap beavers."

"Trap beavers?" said Olavus.

"Yes," said Önde. "Most of the men. And the women and children and the old folk too."

"So you trap beavers," said Olavus, suddenly so excited that his voice sounded like a willow pipe.

"Only the best furs," said Önde. "We can't let Kadis disappear under a mountain of beaver furs and tails."

"And the musk glands?" said Olavus.

"We dry them in bundles in the smoke. And put them in sacks."

"And then?"

"We mix them with the meal for the animals. One sack of musk glands to three sacks of corn. But if anyone wanted to buy a sack we'd probably consider it."

Then Olavus fell on his knees by the wooden bench and thanked God, and he even touched Önde with hands that were almost paralyzed with gratitude.

And as he prayed Önde told him that he might as well wait there in Kadis, the people would be back in a few weeks' time with the beavers, or he could go on somewhere else and return when the musk glands were smoked and dried. He could even stay and help throw the musk glands into sacks. They wove the sacks from the coarsest linen thread.

And Olavus said: "Yes, that will be fine, everything is going to be unbelievably fine." And he drained the beer cup, the beer tasted sweet now with joy and wonder.

So then Önde had to show him round Kadis. Önde dressed up in his rabbitskin hat. And Olavus had to say that Kadis was the most beautiful and most well-ordered place he had seen in the world.

But then he remembered what Könik had said.

"The carpenter, the one planing boards for a coffin, he said that the people were asleep and would soon be getting up again."

"Ah, yes," said Önde, "the beavers are the greatest secret we have here in Kadis, and we never mention them to any stranger."

"But you've told me about them," said Olavus.

"It's different with you," said Önde, "you're going to be staying here in Kadis."

And they went out to see Kadis, the many houses, all the same, oblong and made of stripped pine logs, with birch-bark roofs and an opening for the smoke. Really and truly the houses were nothing special to look at, one single living space with the

29

hearth in the middle of it, a raised hearthstone. And not a single person saw them, because those who were still alive were unwilling to go out, they stayed indoors and sat or lay waiting to die. Even the remaining children had become serious and solemn.

The leather bag containing the gold and silver was so heavy that Olavus had to hold it up with one hand the whole time so that the strap didn't bite too hard into his neck. And Önde took him into houses that were empty and made him try lying on the straw in the abandoned beds and taste the smoked meat that people had left behind when they went out beaver trapping, and sip a little of the beer or the sour milk that had been left out in various places. Yes, the desire to get out into the beaver forests so overwhelmed the people of Kadis that they left everything in a tremendous rush: when the time came they were just up and off, they were taken unawares and struck by beaver frenzy and beaver madness, and they just left their homes and property as suddenly as if they had died.

And he took him to see the chapel, where everything was now so dark that nothing was visible except the cross that Könik had made, and Olavus asked about the priest.

"He's gone after the beavers too," said Önde. "He was among the first to go."

Yes, you could say there was an element of bloodthirstiness in the priest, and he was also indispensable when they made their way into beaver country – it was he who took the lead, and without him the beavers' greatest secrets would never be revealed or understood. He would go on ahead, he had a staff with a cross-piece attached that he held out in front of him, and that staff was like a dowsing-rod, it twisted in his hands, it seemed stronger than the priest, and it pointed straight and unhesitatingly to the beavers' refuge, the hiding-place that was invisible and inaccessible to the powers of human reasoning.

So Önde showed all there was to see in Kadis and told all there was to tell, and they didn't get back to his house till evening.

Olavus was so tired and weak by then that he wanted to go to bed straight away. It had been a wondrous day, and he thanked God for Kadis. When he closed his eyes he could see nothing but beavers' musk glands, piled up like dung-heaps. He would make his way from here down through the whole country with huge linen sacks full to the brim and offering salvation for all – now it was important that he should rest.

But then he started feeling hot, first a pleasant and restful warmth, then burning and irritating, and he had to keep twisting and turning and the straw got crushed beneath him to a fine dust that he breathed in, and painful swellings started to come up in his armpits and groin.

Önde came and sat with him. He had a rabbit's paw in his hand that was actually one of the mother rabbit's front legs, and he dipped the paw in water and bathed Olavus's forehead and cheeks. It felt to Olavus like a woman's fingertips.

And Önde told him about the end of the beaver hunt, and what would happen when the people got back with the kill, which was hauled home on countless sledges made of aspen poles bound together, the way they had done it since time immemorial. The priest would lead the way and the beavers were stacked up and piled high in front of the chapel and the priest sprinkled water on them, and Yvar the smith would hand out the newly-sharpened knives, knives whose handles were made to look like beaver tails, that could never be used for any other purpose than this: cutting out the musk gland. The people would squat on their haunches in front of the chapel and just cut and cut. You had to be careful with the knife so that the liquid didn't run out, the musk itself, and the priest would collect the musk glands in wicker baskets and the baskets would be carried round to the houses and emptied out on to cowhides by the hearth. Next it was the children's job to tie them in bundles so that they could be hung up to be dried and smoked. On the third day they would all stand up, when they had finished cutting the beavers open, and wipe the blood from their hands and scrape the bits of skin and fur and guts off their tunics, and then the great beaver festival would begin. It was a celebration without equal; Kadis was then the most blessed and joyful place on earth. They drank beer by the cupful straight from the vat and danced wild and exciting and frightful dances, in pairs or in great crowds or on their own, whatever they felt like, and there was a great shrieking and stamping on the ground and beaver blood splashed everywhere.

And he talked about all the people, the ones who had gone off but whom he would see again in the celebrations of the festival, he named them by name and described their faces, and as he did so his throat constricted and the words stuck fast before they reached his mouth and his eyes began to run. He had a vision of Jasper in particular, his half-brother, as he had looked when he came home with the rabbit. He was moved to tears by the torment of his own tale.

And they would sing too, they had never forgotten to sing. It was mainly the women who sang, they hummed and swayed the upper part of their bodies to and fro, and then the men would join in, and the singing would flood through Kadis like a giant wall of water. The deepest feeling of bliss comes in singing. "You'll never understand that feeling of elation, Olavus – yes, truly I tell you that you'll soon be with me at the great beaver celebration."

The leather bag lay on Olavus' chest and he was holding on to it with both hands. When he sighed, the gold and silver rattled. But he became quieter and quieter. In the darkness Önde couldn't see him but only hear him. He cried out once, it was as if he had been woken by a sudden pain, and he half sat up and spoke lucidly and intelligently:

"We who are going to live, we who are going to survive, we must have pity on those who will die, we who now will be saved because we have the musk glands of the beaver, we have done so little, we just happen to have been favoured by God's merciful will. We must find joy in life, for there is nothing more precious than life, but we must not forget to pray for those who have to die, for those who have never heard of beaver's musk gland or who are perhaps too poor to buy it – it certainly won't be cheap – we must pray to God to cure them and heal their sickness in eternity or on the Day of the Last Judgement."

Then he collapsed again, his breathing was fast and wheezing, and Önde felt him with his hand. Sweat was pouring down his chest, he had torn off his neckcloth in his effort to cool himself. Önde leaned over and dried him with his coarse, dry hair, he collected up all the sweat in his hair, he pressed and rubbed carefully so that it wouldn't hurt, and his hair was like lichen in the thaw and he had to wring it out on the earth floor.

And finally Olavus went to sleep. Or whatever it was that he was doing now.

Then Önde groped his way across to the other wall and sank down on the cow-fodder, the hay and the leaves, which was where his wife Cecilia had lain while he still had her, and he gave himself up to sleep and to the mercy of God, which in reality he had already attained.

After even the grave-digger had died – and not just the grave-digger but also his sons and his labourer, little lopsided and crooked-legged Ruald who seemed to have been made for standing down in holes and digging – after that it was Könik and Önde who buried people in Kadis. Önde was a strong and fast digger. He often went about it so vigorously that the handle broke, but that was of no great consequence because there were plenty of spades in Kadis now, spades that men had put aside in the ground where they were working and that they had intended to take up again as soon as morning came.

Burying the grave-digger was a worrying business; they weren't as familiar with the technique as he had been. He was a master at the mercy of their novices' clumsiness. They buried him with a feeling of shame, they felt that they were encroaching on his territory, that it wasn't right.

Könik dug with the grave-digger's own spade, and when it was all finished he left the spade standing on the grave. And he thought about how ephemeral man is, even a grave-digger.

After that Könik kept a coffin standing by that he'd made for himself, a coffin that was not to be used by anyone else – no one was going to knock up a crooked and inferior box for him, the expert. And he also made a little coffin for his wife Eira; he put that inside his own, and his mouth went dry and his eyes began to sting when he saw his coffin embracing and concealing hers, that tiny, delicate coffin for a woman, that could equally well have been a child's, inside the rough, strong man's coffin. And he went back in to her, he took a rest from his work for a while and lifted her up in her lameness and embraced her, he enclosed her in his embrace as if he were a cloak or a hiding-place in which she in her frailty could rest safe and secure.

Otherwise Könik and Önde had no time for anything else except trying to keep pace with the Sickness. Önde cut and split timber and dug graves. Könik planed and sawed, and sometimes he dug too, and together they carried out the burials.

That was the most difficult, the actual burials.

Digging the hole and lowering the coffin was easy enough, levering it up and lifting it and bending their backs and groaning, that was simply work for the hands and body and nothing more. But the movements that should be made, the words that should be said, the mysterious incomprehensible words and sounds and the little gestures of head and fingers, all those softly spoken words to send on with the dead that they needed to take with them to their new home in Eternity, words which bonded the ephemeral and the eternal life and even bound death beneath the ground, things that only the priest could perform with real skill, all this caused them fearful difficulties. They were more saddened and depressed by their inability to deal with death in the correct manner than by death itself.

After the priest had died the grave-digger had taken over; he had continued where the priest had left off. He had seen and heard everything on innumerable occasions, it had seemed entirely natural to him – he had even borrowed one of the priest's robes from the chapel, a brown robe with a white cross on the back. He had known for a long time that the step from his own function to that of the priest was infinitesimally small, he may even have thought that his own ability to deal with the eternal and the divine and salvation was just as good as the priest's. He had imitated the priest in a straightforward and competent manner.

Now Könik and Önde were imitating the grave-digger.

It wasn't right. But it wouldn't have been right not to try, to leave the dead unheedingly to their fate.

But they had taken the priest's robe back to the chapel.

They hummed in a low monotone and they spoke words they had never heard before, words which might have any meaning at all, either binding or liberating – that was after they had lowered the coffin into the grave and before they shovelled the earth back in – and they made expansive gestures in the air with their hands. Könik had a bucket of water and a broom and he splashed water over the coffin and the grave and the earth all around.

They thought to themselves that even though God Himself was not there, they would nevertheless turn to Him and invoke His name as best they could.

Groundfrost and God were the most difficult things they had to work with. The groundfrost was nearly three feet deep at the coldest time of winter. Önde found a sharp iron spike at Yvar's smithy and took it, since Yvar didn't need it any more, and he used it to loosen the frozen soil.

And Önde said to Könik: "Perhaps the Sickness and death won't be able to stand the cold."

But Könik didn't know. Perhaps the heat of the summer would burn up the Great Sickness, perhaps the Great Sickness felt at home in the cold, perhaps the Great Sickness was itself the most dreadful coldness, a companion of the ice and the frost and the groundfrost and the northern lights that usually shone over Kadis. So the Great Sickness might be having a good time in the horrors of the winter cold.

They also had to light fires. Not only in their own houses but also in the houses of many a sick person during the short course of the illness; mostly just a brief blaze because everything happened so quickly – there was never any real period of illness to speak of, one moment there was life and the next moment death – fleeting flames in which the dying could see some kind of picture of their own lives. And they lit fires in the houses of others whose fear had rendered them helpless. And Önde lit fires on the ground where he had to dig.

But they never lit a fire in the chapel. There was a hearth in

36

the middle of the floor, but for whom would they have lit a fire? The priest was gone; and as for God, they didn't know. The things the priest had brought with him to Kadis were still there, but neither Könik nor Önde knew how they were used: objects that he had employed to invoke God and set Him in motion, oil and incense and water and bread that he had administered when he shared out God with them. But Könik knew a few words by heart, just a little bit that the priest had taught him, and he used to say those words from time to time, mostly when he was sitting for a while with Eira, who had not moved a single part of her body all winter, or however long a time had now passed like this. Of course God didn't exist in words, but he liked to remember God and to recall the time when the priest was alive and they gathered together in the chapel and everyone lived as they were supposed to live. And he had a little keg of the beer left that Eira had made while she was still on her feet. He would take only enough to cover the bottom of his wooden cup so that he could wet his lips and smell the aroma. Be merciful to us, deliver us, gracious Lord God, from all that is evil, from all that is sinful, from the snares and wiles of the devil, from anger and hatred and all wicked intent and from eternal death.

He wasn't sure whether that was right.

No, why should they have lit a fire in the chapel? They had abandoned that little building, which was nevertheless the biggest in Kadis, to the darkness and the silence and the cold, and thus to God Himself, as Könik had once said.

But from time to time Könik would go in when he passed that way. He would just go in and stand for a while – deliver us gracious Lord God from all evil – and then he might also chance upon someone else there, someone who had simply gone in because he happened to be passing and who was just standing there, and it would immediately seem somehow more frighteningly and uncannily empty; there was a sudden greater awareness of how dreadfully absent something indeterminate actually

37

was, something that they missed painfully and bitterly, yet which, precisely because of that absence and emptiness, almost made its presence felt so tangibly that it could be touched with the hand.

Previously the men used to pee in a particular spot behind the chapel. The snow wouldn't lie there in winter, and in the summer the grass would grow rampant and as high as a man, and they would stand there among the reed-like stalks and the ears of the grass would tickle their mouths and earlobes. It had been like a sanctuary. But now nobody went there, not even Könik, it would have been too painful.

How could they withstand the whole of that winter? If it really was only one winter?

By never letting it seem or feel like a whole long winter, by breaking it up into days and nights and small, short moments, by dividing it up so that it could never be experienced in its entirety and to its terrible full extent. Even the days and moments could be split up and broken down to the size of footsteps one after another, the various little movements of the fingers, the blinking of the eyelids and the breath of the lungs. Like grinding down time in a hand-mill.

That morning when Önde awoke and found that Olavus the trader was dead – yes, he carefully reassured himself that he really was dead, he squeezed him, and closed his eyes as well as he could – he first lit the fire and stirred up some porridge for himself. And when he had eaten he relieved Olavus of all that was weighing him down unnecessarily and that a dead trader can't be expected to have any further use for, and he lifted him up in his arms and carried him out. It was like carrying a log, the trunk of a pine tree.

And although Olavus was heavy, he carried him along the path that went to the chapel, he didn't know why, and took him inside and stood for a while down by the door. Perhaps it might help in some way, and in any case it couldn't do any harm. He did it both for his own and for the dead man's sake. He even tried to remember a word or two that he'd heard the priest say in there, but he couldn't. He had always had a bad memory, had Önde.

Then he went on to Könik's. For the last few yards Olavus became so heavy that he heaved him up on to his left shoulder and held him with both hands round his stiffened knee-joints.

"It's Olavus I've got here," he said to Könik. "That trader fellow."

"Yes," said Könik. "I thought so."

"He should never have come here," said Önde.

"No," said Könik. "It's hard to understand."

"Those who've lived here in Kadis all their lives can't manage to live here any longer," said Önde. "So how could he manage it?"

He had put Olavus down on the carpenter's bench.

"You should have sent him away," said Könik. "You should have told him how things were, that we've got the Great Sickness."

"That was just it," said Önde. "He was so dreadfully afraid of the Great Sickness, he had such a terror of it, that his teeth chattered when he talked about it. So I couldn't bring myself to say it to him."

"You could have saved him. It's your fault that he's lying here now."

Könik had a little wooden mallet in his hand, the mallet he used for his chisel, and he tapped Olavus on the head with it to lend greater weight to his words.

"It was you he came to," said Önde. "It was you who should have sent him away. It was you who should have said how things were. It was you who could have saved him."

"You know as well as I do," said Könik, "that that's not my business. Taking care of strangers who come and don't know their way around."

39

"And you spoke to him. You took the time to talk to him about this and that."

"He wanted to know whether he was in Kadis," said Könik. "And I couldn't deny that."

"No," said Önde.

"And I pointed out the way for him. Because it was to you he had to go."

"I didn't know what to say to him," said Önde. "He was insufferably aggressive and insolent."

"He didn't seem like that to me," said Könik. "Although I didn't really have time even to see him properly."

"And terribly inquisitive about the Great Sickness," said Önde. "He didn't want to talk about anything else. He talked and rattled his teeth, talked and rattled his teeth, that's all he did."

They both looked at Olavus. Könik had two tar-sticks burning. Önde hadn't been able to close his eyes properly.

They had seen that many times now as people died: they lay helpless with their eyes closed, but just as they died they opened them wide, as if the very effort of lifting their eyelids was enough to bring death upon them, as if the business of dying had just been a matter of opening their eyes.

"And I thought," said Önde, "I thought that the only thing I can do is to show him everything. So I took him with me and let him see all the places where the Great Sickness had been."

"Yes," said Könik.

"But I didn't think it was necessary to tell him what he was seeing. He wouldn't have been able to cope with that."

"No," said Könik.

"I wanted to spare him," said Önde. "Because he was filled with such a terrible fear."

Then they fell silent for a good while. They scrutinized Olavus as if they expected him to say something, as if they thought he should have said something to comfort them. Since that was the way things were now.

40

But finally Könik said: "And the money bag? That leather bag?"

Önde seemed not to hear Könik's question about the money bag.

"How are things with Eira?" he asked. "How are you managing with Eira?"

"She's lying where she lies," said Könik.

And he added: "As long as she's lying there lame I don't need to worry too much about her."

"And her food?" said Önde. "And her natural functions?"

"I take care of that," said Könik. "She's like a bird."

Then he asked again about that leather bag that Olavus had had.

"And I thought when I saw it," he said, "that he at least will be able to pay for himself. It's a long time since I got paid for my work. Who'd be able to pay me?"

"I didn't see any money bag round his neck," Önde replied. "The likeliest thing is that he lost it. The leather strap broke and he lost it, especially if it was as full and heavy as you say."

Könik said nothing.

"He was so nervous and uneasy," said Önde. "He would never have noticed it falling off him. In the river. Or in a well. Or in the reeds where no one will find it."

Könik looked at Olavus, it was him he was thinking of. Önde was just the way he was, he was like a twisted spruce – the plane and chisel never went into it the way they should. He was just standing there now feeling for fleas in his beard.

So Könik simply said: "He could have had a piece of silver on each eyelid."

Before Önde went off, before he left Könik and Olavus alone, just as he reached the doorstep, he said: "I've heard that beaver's musk gland is supposed to help."

"Yvar and Ruald both used beaver's musk gland," said Könik. "And they were among the first to die."

And Könik lifted Olavus out of the way so that he could get

to his timber and work on it. He had always used a measuring rod before, but now he made do by eye. And he used to carve loops and tendrils on the lid and long snakes curling round one another, snakes without beginning or end. He'd liked adding them as a little reminder of the beauty of life. Sometimes he had even carved an elegant cross and fixed it to the lid. But now he just made everything as plain as he could. It was as if death had become too big for such childish frills.

And Önde had to talk to someone, he wanted to go to someone who knew nothing about anything, he wanted to talk innocently and frankly with someone.


He went to see Avar.

If you went from Önde's house past the chapel and across the area they called the market-place and then straight on for a hundred paces, you came to Avar's house. After the chapel it was the biggest house in Kadis.

Avar had been an only son and his father had been an only son and both he and his father had married women who were also only children, so he had inherited more than anyone else in Kadis. He was first and foremost an heir. He had sufficient land to feed four cows, and yet he also grew corn, enough to send several loads to Umeå in addition to what was needed for the household and the pigs. He and his wife Tyra had had a son called Egvard who would inherit from him. But then they'd had a daughter – they hadn't meant to – a rosy-cheeked girl with large eyes whom he'd called Ädla. Avar had worried much about what to do with this daughter, since she was unwanted and superfluous, and she ate a lot without getting any fat on her. He had tried to persuade Tyra to lie on her when she was little and smother her. But Tyra was much too thin and light and he wasn't altogether convinced that she had done her best.

But now Tyra and Egvard were both dead; they had gone the

way of all flesh, like most of the others, and Avar was left alone with Ädla, and he loved her very much.

They were sitting inside in the dark when Önde came; there was just a glow in the hearth and it was completely quiet. Avar and Ädla seemed to be sitting there asleep, that was what they mostly did. But Önde picked up a tar-stick and blew on the embers and brought the fire back to life. He liked to have light when he talked.

Then he said that he didn't have any particular reason for calling, he just wanted for once to see a couple of happy people.

Ädla had a fur over her lap and a scraper in her hand. Perhaps she had been sitting there trying to work while half asleep. She was tall and thin, and during the winter she had grown breasts.

"They say you've got enormous bundles of calfskins up in the loft," said Önde.

Avar looked up rather cautiously and said: "Well, yes."

"And I've heard that you've got enough dried fish for several years, as if you had ten mouths to feed."

"That might be so," said Avar.

"And enough iron for spades and spits and axes by the hundred."

Now Avar straightened up.

"I haven't counted them as exactly as all that," he said.

"And a cow-shed," said Önde. "And eight animals."

"Ten," said Avar. "You forgot the pig. And a suckling calf."

"Well," said Önde. "I can only say that it surpasses my understanding."

"What surpasses my understanding," said Avar, raising himself up so that he was standing on the floor, "is that there are people who can live empty-handed. Destitute and without inheritance."

"Yes," said Önde, "you never need to dread the coming day."

"And yet," said Avar, lighting another stick and pushing it into the edge of the fire, "and yet there's a lot you don't

43

remember, and a lot you never knew. Now that you're talking about what's mine."

"Of course," said Önde. "But everyone knows that you've got huge amounts of things that no one knows about."

"There are also things that are hidden out in the forest," said Avar, "things that are so well hidden that not even a ferret could find them."

He was standing in the middle of the floor now and waving his arms about, talking slowly but ardently, and nodding his head with every word. And the two tar-sticks shone splendidly upon him.

"Not to mention what might lie hidden here and there in the ground," he went on. "Leather bags and tin boxes and wooden chests. When it comes down to it you know hardly anything, Önde."

"No," said Önde. "I don't think I know very much. And even then we always know a lot less than we think we do."

"I'm not saying that all the things actually exist," Avar said – and now he was so excited and animated that he was stuttering – "but I'll still tell you what might be found, and you can reckon out the rest yourself. There might be silver plates like the palm of your hand. And there might be copper bars as big as horses' heads. And there might be translucent pieces of unknown substances, both red and green. And there might be gold coins with pictures on them of kings and queens and serpents."

And then he fell silent.

"Now I've probably said too much," he said. "And still I haven't said everything. Far from it."

And he sat down again – perhaps he was tired after talking so much and so fervently.

"You ought to know," he said, "you ought to know, Önde, that there might be just about anything at all."

There they sat; Önde too had sat down on a stool by the door, and the charcoal fire shone on them and they thought about all that silver and gold and all the copper and all the precious stones

44

that there might be, those possible riches. They thought long and hard, Ädla distractedly rubbing the scraper on the pelt, and completely unexpectedly Önde began to cry. He was surprised himself when he felt the tears running down his cheeks and nose. He might be a big, tall, coarse and ugly man, but sometimes he wept amazingly copious tears.

And when Avar noticed it, he said thoughtfully:

"Well, well, Önde."

Önde had trouble in speaking, he had phlegm in his throat and his voice croaked shakily and haltingly as he said: "I'm sitting here thinking about who will take care of all those things there might be, who will keep a check on what there is and what there may be and separate it from what there has never been, who will do it all when you are gone, Avar."

And Avar turned his head towards him immediately and said very loud and clear:

"Ädla will do it."

And now Önde talked about what he knew, about the things he'd felt compelled to talk about to someone, about what Olavus the trader had told him, that it must definitely be the Great Sickness that was raging in Kadis – yes, not just in Kadis but everywhere where people lived, that it was also called the Wrath of God, especially the sort that had struck Kadis and that killed the sick in one day or one night, the sort that really wasn't a sickness at all but that consisted solely of death and destruction, death in its purest form.

As he was talking, the first of the tar-sticks, the one Önde had lit when he arrived, went out, and Avar, who had till then looked really tall and well-fed and straight-backed, seemed to shrink a little in the dark. And three rabbits came out from where they had been lying in comfort under Ädla's skirt and started chewing the barley straw that covered the floor.

Yes, it seemed likely that the earth would be wiped clean of heirs, or at least no one would be able to know for certain who would finally turn out to be the heir. The Great Sickness took over all property and possessions and gave them in the end to whoever it wanted, to anyone at all. Whole families who had lived and bred moderately and peacefully for generation after generation would be wiped out. Perhaps new families would arise, but even that was uncertain. Individuals pairing off at random couldn't create families of the old type, a family was something that was bred with foresight and calculation. Yes, Avar knew that well, in a family all were chosen, they weren't just conceived and born, they were made to measure and created for the ineffably high purpose that the family represented.

Two of the rabbits were mating now, they were coupling beneath the stick that was still burning. Önde and Avar and Ädla watched them and said nothing, they didn't want to disturb them. There was something solemn and moving in what the rabbits were doing.

Then Önde continued: Probably Avar knew all this already, he didn't imagine that he was revealing any secrets, but for him it had been as if his eyes had been opened when he listened to that trader Olavus, when he heard those very words "the Great Sickness" and "God's Exceeding Wrath", when he had described for him everything that he already knew deep inside himself. And there was no cure, everything had been tried, from beetle dung to beaver's musk gland, but nothing helped. In the richest city in the world – he couldn't remember right now what the city was called – well, that didn't really matter – people there had had remedies sent from all over the world. As soon as they heard of a possible cure they sent carts and wagons to fetch it. They had bought or grabbed for themselves everything that might possibly save them. But now the city had died out, not a single living soul was left, all that remained were enormous mounds of remedies and cures.

Now the second tar-stick had also burned out and Avar was huddled up again in the dark by the wall.

This Olavus had said that if they wanted to get the better of

46

the Great Sickness, they had to be cunning and do something unexpected. It wasn't enough to let the days go by and think that their cure and salvation was to be found in the familiar and the ordinary, in things that had been adequate and useful since time immemorial, in simple manual tasks and the eternally-repeated daily round and in their morning and evening porridge. No, if there was any salvation at all, then it must lie in some terrible aberration or unnatural practice, so they would have to think up something that no one had dared to think of before in Kadis.

At least, that was how Olavus the trader had explained it.

Where was this Olavus, where could he meet him and exchange a few words with him, Avar asked.

But that wasn't possible any more, he was no longer there in Kadis; he had just stocked up with a few necessities, some clothes and a few loaves, and then gone on his way. No one but God knew where he was now.

And Avar wouldn't have been able to get any more out of Olavus than what he, Önde, had told him now. Önde had repeated everything, he had probably added a few things that Olavus himself hadn't been aware of. The truth, said Önde, the truth in what people said always included more than the people themselves could imagine.

And then Önde had to go. He had a cow to look after and he had to keep Könik supplied with timber and he had to lay a fire for some poor folk who were helpless and unable to look after themselves.


Könik had seen Önde go to Avar's. He had even followed him part of the way to make sure that he really did bend down and go in and close the door after him. Then he went to Önde's house.

He owed himself that. And Olavus. And Önde. It was no more than was right. If he'd been able to think of something more than was right, he would have gone there when Önde was at home and demanded it.

He didn't need a light. He had a little iron hook in his hand that Yvar had once made him for some purpose that he'd now forgotten.

When he came in he went past the hearth and over to the cow – there was pale-blue smoke rising from the ashes, it was alder wood – and he pushed the cow away with his body so that he could get to the spot on the floor where she always stood. Then he started digging with the iron hook.

How did he know it was here he should look?

He knew Önde, he had known him since they were little and had hidden birds' eggs and snails from one another.

Önde wanted never to forget anything. So he chose hiding-places that he wouldn't forget.

Önde used to say: "One day I'll have a casket with golden fittings." The nearest you could get to a golden casket was the earth under the cow. Sometimes Önde would be overcome by an incomprehensible and irrational fear, and then he used to hide under the cow's belly.

So Könik didn't need to dig for long before the iron hook caught on something soft yet firm. That's how it had always been with Önde, if no one forced him to dig deep he would just dig a hasty shallow hole. Könik put the iron hook aside and used his fingers, and soon lifted up the leather bag, which was even heavier than he'd imagined. It was drawn together with the leather thong that Olavus had had round his neck, the thong was threaded through holes cut in the leather and tied in a double-looped knot. Könik untied the knot: it came quickly and easily – he even knew Önde's knots of old.

He put his hand down into the bag, he let his fingers wander freely among the riches, it was like putting his fingertips into soft sand.

Then with his thumb and forefinger he picked out two coins, not too big, but not too small either, two smooth round coins.

48

Two silver coins, that was what Olavus owed him. He was sure that if he had asked Olavus what the right price for a splendid coffin would be, Olavus would have said without hesitation: Two moderately large silver coins.

And he pushed them in under his tongue, that's what he used to do with things that were small and fragile; he even used to put the little piece of bread that the priest gave out at Mass under his tongue, and it would stay there until it dissolved and disappeared. That was his hiding-place: under the tongue.

Then he tied up the leather bag again and put it back into the hole and covered it over. He would have liked to dig it down deeper and safer, but he couldn't do that because of Önde.

When he got back home he lit the fire, and spat out the coins on his carpenter's bench.

And then he saw that they were not white but golden yellow, they were not silver but almost certainly gold. He had never seen gold before. Olavus had made a mistake, a simple error because it was so dark inside Önde's house, and had paid him in gold coins.

And it was probably now that everything really began, the slide into fiction: a brief attack of delirium and confusion, the beginning of a fever or trance; and he rubbed his forehead with his shirt-sleeves and pressed his thumbs against his eyes.

He stood for a long time staring at the gold coins. He forgot that he ought to go and look after Eira. This was more than was right. Olavus the trader would have had to say: Look here, I'll provide for everything, I'll pay for the burial of everyone in Kadis, all the dead who owe you something, I'll release them from their debts.

At last he went in anyway and fed Eira and told her about everything that was still alive and moving in Kadis and lifted her a little so that she wouldn't get bedsores. She really felt like a bird.

Then he stood working on the lid of Olavus' coffin all evening. He carved tendrils and loops and mighty serpents curling around one another, he tried to create something that would be worth at least a little sliver of gold, and finally he carved an elegant cross and nailed the lid down.

Before he went to sleep that night – and he found it terribly difficult nowadays to get to sleep – he hid the two gold coins beneath Eira, in the warmth under her left shoulder-blade. He had wrapped them up in the neck fur of a rabbit.

After Önde had gone it was quiet in Avar's house for some while. Every time Ädla was about to fall asleep where she sat, she was awoken by the noise of the scraper rubbing against the pelt on her lap or a crackling from the charcoal in the hearth.

Avar had pulled a sheepskin over his shoulders and was leaning back against the wall. From time to time it sounded as if he were snoring, but he wasn't asleep. When no one was looking at him he was in the habit of letting his chin drop forward on to his chest.

Ädla usually never said a word. Avar jumped when he heard her voice. It was slightly shrill and complaining.

"And who will take care of the rabbits?" she said, as if they had already been talking to one another. She had made a sort of hut, a pen, from her dead mother's tunic, and she had four rabbits in it.

"The rabbits," said Avar, "God will look after them. They're not aware of death, they'll save themselves."

"At night they come and lie against my belly," Ädla said. "And I give them aspen leaves."

"You mustn't worry about the rabbits," said Avar. "It's a sin to think about the rabbits. We must just think of ourselves."

"What is there about me to think of?" said Ädla. "All I do is sit here. Except when I'm milking and soothing the cows.

"But the rabbits," she added, "they're like a creator, they have so much love that they can never be at rest."

She was remembering what Jasper had said when he came back with the mother of all the rabbits, the doe he called Maria.

"Everything that exists," said Avar, "is there for mankind's sake. The earth and the sky and the sun. And of course rabbits too. When we think of ourselves our concern benefits the whole of creation."

Ädla was silent for quite a long time, and then she said: "It feels to me as if it were exactly the opposite."

"You're blaspheming," said Avar, "you're rebelling against God. If you weren't my own flesh and blood I'd hit you with the pig-stick." He had a gnarled and knotty stick for hitting the pigs with. They seldom went where he wanted them to go, and he said it was good for the meat.

"But you're only a child," he went on to say. "You know hardly anything. No, what you know would fit on to the nail of my little finger."

Ädla fell silent. It was true that she knew nothing, she had never wanted to know anything in particular, she had seen Avar being tormented by all he knew.

"But there are some things that you have to know," said Avar.

And Ädla said nothing, she just made a few scraping motions on the pelt – she didn't really know how to scrape a pelt, but she did it nevertheless.

"Do you hear me talking to you?" said Avar.

"Yes. I'm listening."

"There are things that you must know, even if I have to use force," said Avar.

"Yes," said Ädla. "I know."

"You must know," said Avar, "that there are five silver spoons under the pig-pen, three feet deep, right under the food trough."

"Yes," said Ädla, and it almost sounded as if she already knew.

"And in the cow-shed, in the corner by the iron pot, there's a hollow log – the fourth log up from the bottom, and in it there's a sheepskin and in the sheepskin there are some silver coins."

"Yes."

"And under the rowan tree by the barley-drying shed there's a leather pouch with ten gold coins in it."

"Under the actual roots?" Ädla asked.

"Yes. I put the pouch there first and then planted the rowan.

"And you also ought to know," he continued, "that there's a similar bag here under the threshold too."

"Yes."

"And there's a hollowed-out space in the wooden block you're sitting on. And there I've put pieces of translucent stone, red and green."

Ädla got up and moved to the stool on which Önde had sat.

"And under the altar stone in the chapel there are five gold coins. I gave them to the priest. He promised us happiness and gave us his blessing. The money itself doesn't belong to us, but the happiness and blessing do."

"Yes."

"And that axe hanging on the wall that no one is allowed to use – that's not made of iron but of silver. I've hidden that by keeping it visible."

Then he fell silent and let his chin drop towards his chest and seemed to doze off and start snoring.

"Is that all I have to know?" asked Ädla.

"No one else in the whole of Kadis knows as much as that," said Avar.

And he dozed off once again. Ädla put down the pelt and scraper on the earth floor and picked up one of the rabbits that was running around at her feet. It was a little doe, really just a baby, but it was already pregnant.

Then Avar sighed, almost as if talking to himself: "Now I've cast off earthly things. Now I'm ready to die."

He stood up and put a couple of pieces of wood on the fire and blew some life into the embers, and when the fire had caught he said: "If I think about what Önde said, it makes my whole body tremble."

"What was it that Önde said, then?" asked Ädla.

"You heard him yourself."

"Önde," said Ädla. "Who would be silly enough to take any notice of what Önde says?"

"He's the most honourable man I know," said Avar. "Önde would never be able to speak an untrue word."

They hadn't eaten anything since their midday porridge. But neither of them thought of food, as often happened.

"If Önde says that the sickness here in Kadis is called the Great Sickness, then that's what it is. If he calls it the Dread Wrath of God, then that's what it is. And if he says that all heirs will be the first to be purged from the surface of the earth, then that's what will happen."

Ädla stroked the rabbit.

"But I don't think it really means very much to die," he said.

Then he raised his voice, and clenched his fists and screamed at her: "If we both die, then the silver spoons and leather pouches will be without an owner. Ordinary folk may die as they will but the family mustn't die, the gold and the silver and the fields and the bundles of pelts and happiness and blessing and the ironware – they need someone to stay alive and own them. This house must never lack an heir."

Then he calmed down again. He sat down and propped his chin on his knuckles and said: "I must think more about this aberration that Önde was talking about, we must do something that the Sickness has not foreseen, something absolutely preposterous, something to hit death on the head and stop it in its tracks."

"When I hear you say that, my whole body begins to tremble," said Ädla.

"I'm looking at the rabbits," said Avar. "They're a kind of creator, they breed incessantly to avoid death."

"You shouldn't concern yourself with the rabbits," said Ädla. "It's a sin to think about rabbits."

"They can never be without heirs," said Avar.

"No," said Ädla. "What they've got, they'll surely possess for all eternity."

"I'll create an heir in you," said Avar. "It's disgusting, but it's necessary. That's what I'll do. The Sickness can't have foreseen that. I'll beget an heir in you."

Ädla turned so pale and wan that her face began to shine in the dark.

"But think of yourself," she said. "Think of what you would do to yourself."

"What is there about me to think of?" said Avar. "All I do is sit here, except when I'm carrying wood or slaughtering some poor animal."

Since Thomas the butcher had died it was Avar who did the slaughtering in Kadis. He had a wooden club with a sharpened iron spike in the end.

"Everything that exists is there for mankind's sake," said Ädla, and she was slurring her words a little because her lips and tongue had gone stiff and numb with fear. "So men should not behave like the animals."

"To me," said Avar, "it feels as if it were exactly the opposite."

"You're blaspheming," said Ädla, "you're rebelling against God. Remember that I'm your own flesh and blood."

"If I die and if you die, the heir will live," said Avar. "We must save our inheritance from being ownerless and forgotten."

"And I'm only a child," said Ädla, "I don't know anything, and what I do know would fit on the nail of your little finger."

"I shall teach you," said Avar. "I shall do exactly the same as when I made our heir Egvard and when I made you."

"I've never even thought about it," said Ädla, "how mankind reproduces itself."

"I shall teach you," said Avar. "I shan't use force."

"I'll be the one that has to use force," said Ädla. "You'll make me use force against myself."

Then he stood up and got himself ready for the night; and he went to bed – but she didn't follow.

So Avar got up and fetched her. He took her by the hair and brought her to the bed. And she lay with him, though really she didn't know what to do when a woman lies with a man.

So he taught her. It was an unbearable pain for him to do it, it was so repellent that he could see that the Great Sickness would seem nothing by comparison, and she cried and didn't understand what he meant her to do, and at the same time as he was teaching her he was climbing on to her and doing it.

Many people lay dead or dying in Kadis while this was going on. They were delirious with fever, most of them did not know what was happening to them, they had forgotten what they used to be called, and here they will not even be named by name.

Evan, Thomas the butcher, Signhild and Orov and Tjalve and many, many others. But Kadis itself went on, it was changing but was still whole and entire, all that had existed was still there.

And Könik was caring for Eira, who still lay unmoving in her bed. He fed her and kept her clean and warm as well as he could, and he told her that hardly anyone was dying any more now.

"I'll soon be making carts and sledges and yokes and boats and fox traps again," he said.

And as if to confirm his words, Avar came to see him and said he would like a cradle made, a cradle to hang from a roof beam, a swinging chair for a little baby – yes, for a child not yet born. He said it to make Könik ask him who could possibly be having a baby now.

And Könik was indeed astonished.

"Who is it who's going to have a baby now?" he said.

"It's Ädla," said Avar.

And Könik could not help asking who had been the cause.

"It was a trader called Olavus," said Avar. "He was a fatally restless soul, he suddenly appeared from nowhere and caused this."

And where was he now, Könik asked, this trader Olavus? For it was not long ago that he had put up a special stake on Olavus' grave, a stake on which he had carved the shape of a leather bag. He hadn't the heart to tell Avar that.

"He went on his way," said Avar. "He didn't have the patience to wait until the baby was due, and he probably couldn't be expected to. Who can have patience in times like these?"

"So you'll have an heir after all," said Könik.

"Yes," said Avar, straightening up proudly, "it's not God's will that my family should be extinguished from the face of the earth. And who the father of a child is doesn't mean much either. The child is itself, if it lives it will be its own man or woman. A father doesn't create a child, he just calls it forth from out of the darkness. A father is no more than a chisel or a hook or a pair of pliers."

He said that in a very loud voice, both to himself and to Könik.

And at the same time he put his hands over his groin as if to cover it – although he was wearing both a tunic and a leather apron – or as if he had suddenly got a terrible pain right there.

Könik realized immediately what sort of child it was that Avar and Ädla were expecting.

"Nevertheless it's strange," he said, "how common it is for children to resemble their fathers. As if you could see the marks left by the chisel or pliers. Or the hook."

Avar was quiet for a moment then. He looked at the timber and the carpenter's bench and the tools and the walls, but not at Könik. And he remembered the priest. So he said:

"The priest used to say that children get their bodies from their mother but marrow and soul from their father. I wonder if that's really how it is."

"Yes," said Könik. "That's how it is."

"In fact we know nothing at all," said Avar, now sounding quite miserable. He was almost shivering.

And Könik's thoughts turned quickly to Eira. And to Önde and Olavus and the chapel and Ädla – indeed, to the whole of Kadis.

"No," he said, "there's nothing we can know for certain."

He would never have been able to say anything like that about Kadis before.

Then he said that he would make the swinging cradle, but that there were one or two things he had to do first, and there probably wasn't any burning hurry. And Avar said that the cradle should be made so that Ädla could fasten him in, the heir, if he was a restless soul, that he oughtn't to be able to wander off and he should sit securely – yes, if he had to be left alone for some reason that he couldn't foresee and which he'd rather not talk about, then he should be able to sit there until he was old enough to climb down and take possession of his inheritance. Könik brought out two skinned rabbits – you can't eat an unlimited amount of rabbit meat, he said – and he wanted to send them over to Ädla. She ought to eat to stop her strength ebbing away before she gave birth; after all, she was only a child herself. And for a man, he said, this meat has a strangely sweet taste after a while.

And before Avar left, Könik told him something that Önde had spoken about, just a little story about the Great Sickness – a story is the best way of ending a conversation, so that you can go away with an easy mind:

A man had noticed that all the animals stayed healthy, the cows and sheep and goats and pigs: in some way they were immune, the Sickness and death didn't bother with them. So he got a cowhide and put it on, a hide with the hooves still on it and the head and the ears; he pulled it on and made himself into a cow and went off to a stall in the cow-shed. He stood there on all fours and became an animal, he ate hay and leaves and drank out of the water trough. The folk in his house died one after another, but he chewed his hay and even learned how to moo; the only thing he couldn't do was to give milk. The Sickness and death thought that he looked like an ordinary cow; he chewed the cud and felt safe, filled with and redeemed by the mighty strength imbued by his cunning. But there was a pig

59

there rubbing and scratching itself in the pen next to his stall, and it stabbed its eye on a branch – it bled frightfully and the pig shrieked and squealed horribly and rushed around in its pen in panic. The man who was a cow couldn't help seeing it and hearing it. He could feel himself how it would hurt to pierce your eye, he became more and more desperate and tormented at hearing the pig cry and wail, and finally he could contain himself no longer: he mooed in sympathy and straightened himself and stood upright so that the cowhide slipped off him – he had to try to help and console the pig. But then the Sickness saw that he was a man, his human qualities were immediately obvious and incontestable, and before nightfall his blood turned feverish and he only lived for one more day.

This was during the late winter. Önde was able to walk on the frozen snow and set snares for birds and hares; and sometimes by chance he would catch a rabbit.

Many possessions had now become ownerless in Kadis. People left land and houses and property: at the beginning there were always heirs, but as time went on even they became fewer. What Önde had said about heirs began to come true.

For those still living it was shocking to see how earthly things were simply abandoned.

But there was always some reason why they should really be the heirs themselves.

Evan's fields down by the river were wrongly marked out, said Avar. "They've always been wrongly divided, they've really always belonged to us."

Borne, called the executioner but really a kindly man, said that Yvar's house was now his. If Yvar's widow had lived she would have taken him – he had lain with her once.

In those days when the need still arose it was Borne who had chopped the heads off the condemned or hanged them. He was responsible for the little house called the lock-up. He used to take care of the animals that died a natural death and he had looked after the big rat traps. Everyone felt an uncertain and indeterminate fear of him, as well as a strange sort of liking for him. It was his job to whip those who had to be whipped, and then care for them afterwards. He was big and thick-set, in fact he was the burliest man in Kadis. He had fair hair that hung down in curls over his cheeks, and he always smiled, whatever he was doing. But he didn't have a woman.

So he had now inherited Yvar's house. No one, not even he himself, could see what he wanted it for.

Previously, Könik had taken timber from the common land, and now he let the forests that had belonged to the dead join up with the common, and somehow they came to be his. Especially where the pines were branchless.

Önde also soon came into an inheritance. From Thomas the butcher he got knives and the hammer that Avar didn't want and two beer kegs and a box of hooves to boil the glue out of. Thomas left only one survivor, a baby girl still in the cradle. Önde took her home to his house so that she could die in the warm with his cow. So it was her inheritance that became his.

But Avar was by far the worst. It wasn't just Evan's fields that fell to his lot, he also allowed himself to inherit the chapel. He had performed acts at least as mysterious and wonderful as the priest's. "When all of you others are dead, my family will need the chapel as a storehouse for their inheritance."

But then Avar got the Sickness.

He woke up one morning in a fever and didn't get up from his bed. By midday he had the first pustules on his neck. Ädla held a burning stick over him and saw them rising up like bubbles on fermenting beer. And Avar knew that he was going to die.

"It doesn't bother me," he said. "Now that I know there'll be someone after me."

"I shall kill him the moment he's born," said Ädla.

61

"You won't be able to," said Avar. "You'll give him your breast. You're no different from other women."

His tongue had swollen, and although he was speaking even more slowly than usual his speech was slurred.

Ädla felt her breasts, they were heavy and aching.

"A daughter shouldn't bear her father's child," she said. "You tricked me, you tricked this child into me."

"One child is as good as another," said Avar. "The main thing is that a life is conceived, the only thing that counts is life; how life comes into existence is not important."

But now Ädla told him a story that he didn't know. It was Önde who had told her, he had come over just to tell it to her. She didn't look at Avar and she spoke with tight lips, hardly moving her lower jaw:

In Umeå there was a son who had fathered a child on his own mother. He had done it without her noticing as she knelt at her loom weaving a braid that was so complicated that she was in a kind of trance, as if far away and deaf to everything. But she realized later what must have happened, she had been a widow for many years living alone with her son, and she knew what they must both have done in their folly. She questioned her son and he immediately admitted it: he had obviously not known what he was doing, the whole deed was so involved that he had been as if in a trance. She herself certainly bore no responsibility for what had happened, not for her own part, since she had been in a kind of daze, but she was of course responsible for what she had done through her son, in the person of her son.

So she went to one of the priests in Umeå and disclosed everything in tears.

It was nothing new or unknown for the priest, but even so he felt so moved that he wept too; he had never thought that he himself would encounter a phenomenon that was so talked about and serious and fateful, and he blessed the woman and thanked her for coming specifically to him. He knew so dreadfully well what had to be done.

62

And he made sure that it was done.

They fetched the son and clapped him in irons. And then they cut open the mother and pulled out the child. The priest foretold what they would find, and that was exactly what they did find.

The child – if it really was a child – had a head as big as its body and its eyes were those of a frog; it had long hair on all its limbs and it had gills just like a fish below its cheeks.

And they cut the mother and son into little pieces and burned them bit by bit on a huge fire in Umeå, in order to redeem them, and they threw the child into the river so that it could swim with the other water-creatures.

That, or something like it, was the story Ädla told to Avar.

"Yes," said Avar, "that was totally repulsive. A son with his own mother. Man's lechery knows no bounds."

"Yes," said Ädla, "they certainly did the right thing in Umeå. And in Umeå they have all the knowledge in the world. But they should have punished them harder still."

"How could they have punished them any harder?" Avar asked.

"I don't know," said Ädla. "I don't know anything. What I know would fit on to the nail of your little finger."

"And why did you tell me this story?" said Avar. "Right now when I'm about to die."

"Because," said Ädla, "because it's exactly the same as you did to me."

Avar was silent for a few moments, as if he was resting. Then he said:

"It really is true that you don't know anything. I'm not just anyone. It was, me, Avar, who did that to you. I'm your own father. I can't be compared with strangers in Umeå."

"Yes, that's right, you're my father," said Ädla. "You could equally well have done it with your own mother."

"The human race reproduces itself forwards," said Avar. "Begetting children with your own mother, that's reproducing backwards."

"Fathers and mothers and sons and daughters and brothers and sisters shouldn't feel carnal lust for each other," said Ädla.

"I didn't do it because of lust but because of my torment," said Avar.

"Önde says that children can't be conceived without lust," said Ädla, "it's lust that sets off the actual conception."

"Who would be stupid enough to take any notice of what Önde says?" said Avar.

"He's the most honest man I know," said Ädla. "Önde would never be able to speak an untrue word."

Then they fell silent. But after a while Ädla said:

"I shall still kill the child and heir the moment he's born, in fact if I'm able to I'll kill him while he's being born, in the very act of birth."

"If you do that," said Avar, "then God will send the devil to punish you, he'll burn you up bit by bit on a fire."

But then he wanted to speak to Önde; Ädla had to go and fetch him, and quickly too, because he didn't know how much longer he could continue to put off the moment of death.

So Ädla brought Önde over.

And Avar explained to Önde – and this was now his last will and testament – that he, Önde, was to act as a guardian to Ädla and the heir, he was to take Avar's place. The trouble with Ädla was that she lacked common sense, and someone had to look after her and watch over what she did. Of course she usually preferred doing nothing, but sometimes he had seen in her eyes that she was sitting thinking out things that she could do, and that had filled him with an irrational dread.

Önde nodded and said yes. Respect for death made him taciturn.

Yes, by and large Ädla was just a temporary solution to the problem of life. In herself she was insignificant, she would simply fill the void between himself and the heir. All Önde could do was watch over her to stop her trying to make herself out to be anything more or greater than life's temporary expedient.

64

While Avar was talking to Önde, Ädla noticed that one of the rabbits was in the act of giving birth to its young in the bed it had made of her mother's skirt. And she went and sat with the rabbit.

Önde wasn't to think that he had to take pity on Ädla for nothing. No, Avar had five gold coins in his chapel, under the big stone altar. Önde was to take one of them, but only when he had fulfilled all his obligations to Ädla and the heir. He was to borrow a pair of Yvar's pincers and cut the coin across the centre, and he could keep one half for ever, the gold half-coin would belong to him and his descendants.

"I don't have any descendants," said Önde.

"If it turns out," said Avar, "that you never have any descendants, then I want you to put that piece of gold back before you die."

But Önde thought that this last desire of Avar's was so grandiose and at the same time so difficult to carry out that he decided immediately never to bother himself about that gold half-coin.

And then Avar wanted to exchange a few words with Könik, and Önde had to go and fetch him.

Ädla sat with the rabbit that was giving birth, helping her, and when the baby rabbit was born — it was just a single one — she picked it up and held it in her hands, making a little nest for it in the palms of her hands.

When Könik came he squatted down by Avar, who was getting weaker all the time, moving gradually closer to death. And Ädla got up and came over to them and opened her hands so that they could see the baby rabbit. It had two heads and three back legs.

"What's that?" said Avar.

"It's the baby rabbit that's just been born," said Ädla.

"It's got two heads and three back legs," said Avar.

"Yes," said Ädla.

"That's inbreeding," said Könik.

Avar said nothing.

"All the rabbits here in Kadis," Könik went on, "come from the same seed and the same womb. It's brothers and sisters and fathers and mothers that are mating with each other."

But Avar didn't want to talk about the baby rabbit: he was busy dying.

"Take it away," he told Ädla, "it reminds me of something fateful and horrible, but I've forgotten what it is."

No, he wanted to talk to Könik about the coffin.

It wasn't even necessary to have the usual sort of coffin, it would be good enough to put a few rough boards round him and hold them together with a couple of barrel hoops. He would like everything to be as simple as possible. Death was insignificant as far as he was concerned. Ädla would pay Könik later for it, and for the swinging seat for the heir. He had put aside a bundle of calfskins that were in good condition on the whole, even though the maggots had eaten them a little bit round the edges. But he knew that Könik was a good-natured man who was always pleased with whatever people gave him.

And Könik should know that he'd asked Önde to be Ädla's guardian, so he wanted Könik to keep an eye on Önde.

Yes, of course he would, said Könik. He'd tried for a long time to keep an eye on Önde, as far as it was possible.

Before Avar died Könik wanted to tell him that he hadn't expected this, he hadn't thought that Avar would die. Death was always senseless, but Avar's death was the most senseless of all.

Könik was having to whisper. He was really so upset that his voice failed him. It felt as if he was sitting at his own father's deathbed again, as if this were the death of all fathers in Kadis.

And he tried to explain it to Avar. He searched long and uncertainly among the words that he could remember.

It seemed to him that Avar represented what had been right and proper in Kadis, the order that had always prevailed. The men of Kadis had known from time immemorial how things should be, they had known it in themselves, they had gathered together and agreed on what was permitted and what was for-

66

bidden and what was mine and what was yours, and they had seen to it that anyone who did something unlawful rather than what was lawful received his punishment, and anything that had been upset or gone astray or gone wrong they had restored to its rightful place. They had had the true knowledge.

Yes, Avar was the last one to embody law and justice.

And if they themselves did wrong, they also judged themselves.

But those times had gone now. This was the only father left, and Könik felt a terrible dread when he thought about the confusion and disorder that was coming. Yes, he had often consoled himself in recent times with the thought that Avar was still there, the only one left of the grey-haired and white-bearded ones. When all who were going to die had finally died, they would still be able to ask Avar about the original order of things, about the principles for re-establishing what was right and proper.

That, or something like it, was what Könik tried to say in a whisper to Avar. That when he went, all that was pure and genuine in Kadis would be lost too.

But Avar probably didn't hear it all, his senses were fading. Könik knew from the smell of him and the warmth he exuded that he really was dying, and he told Ädla that he was dying now. Ädla came creeping over to them, still with the baby rabbit in her hands. They listened to his breathing, heavy and irregular. Könik thought: I'll sit here until he stops breathing. As long as he was breathing Kadis was still the same as it was meant to be.

Then Ädla said in a calm but rather sharp voice: "What is it that's happening inside him now?"

For something seemed to be happening, he was shaking so much that the air around him was set in motion as if by a gust of wind, and it sounded as if a whistling or a whimpering noise was coming from inside his chest. Then he heaved a great sigh, deep and groaning and decisive, and Ädla and Könik both thought that this was the moment of death.

67

But what was really happening was the opposite: he began to shake his head so that the straw crackled and he flailed his arms as if there was something he had to beat off and he kicked his legs as if he was trying to get up and run off to God knows where.

Then he lay still again, but was clearly and obviously alive.

"It's dreadful," he said pitifully. "It's so awful that I had to wake up."

"What is it that's so dreadful and awful?" asked Ädla.

"I never thought I'd ever have to experience such terror," said Avar.

"What is it that's so terrifying?" asked Könik.

"What I did with Ädla," said Avar. "What I did with my own flesh and blood. What I did in my shameful madness."

Then all three of them were silent for a while.

"Yes," said Könik. "It's certainly terrifying."

"I have offended against the natural order of things," said Avar.

"You thought you were doing something natural," said Könik. "But there is something that is perhaps even more natural." It was a dreadful thing for Könik as well, and momentarily it almost felt as if he too had carried out Avar's deed. That's what men had kept a check on up till now in Kadis: the natural order of things.

"If I die," said Avar, "I'll go to hell because of what I've done."

And Könik tried to look at Ädla, as if he thought she might have said: "No, you won't go to hell." But she said nothing.

"Yes," said Könik. "You probably can't escape hell."

If only the priest had still been alive. Although that probably wouldn't have helped either.

"He might be stillborn," said Ädla. "The heir. And he needn't be at all like this little rabbit."

"That's neither here nor there," said Avar. "Whether he comes out of you alive or dead, and however many heads he has, I'm damned in any case."

68

Nothing more was said. Neither Ädla nor Könik knew what to say. It was still clear that Avar was going to die, and they had no advice to give him and no oil to rub on him and no soothing or consoling words. And Könik had to go home to Eira: she didn't know where he was. That was her only occupation: waiting for Könik.

When Könik had gone Ädla huddled up in her bed, holding the rabbit against her cheek. It died in the night.

Avar dozed off too. He fell asleep quickly, breathing shallowly as the dying often did. But he didn't die, he simply didn't dare to die. His fear was his salvation.

That evening Könik said to Eira: "Soon all who are going to die will have died. Apart from Avar nobody is sick any more in Kadis, so you can get better again too."

And he told her that the sow Evan had left had farrowed, a single piglet, and he thought he would look after it, he and Eira. It was the largest piglet he'd seen in his whole life, a boar.

*Over all our deeds there hangs*
*a veil of trance.*

When all those who were going to die had died, there were seven left alive in Kadis. They were Könik and Eira and Önde and Borne, called the executioner, and Bera, who had never had any teeth. She lived by the gap in the fence that was known as the village gate, and she kept goats and made cheese and used to make meals for the priest. A person can be afflicted even by that: never growing any teeth. She was the same age as Könik's Eira. They had shared a doll when they were little, a doll that Eira's mother had made from a squirrel pelt and hair from cows' tails, and they had learned to milk together. They also lost their milk teeth at the same time as one another and they kept them and made them into a necklace for the doll. But after that Bera didn't grow any new teeth, her gums stayed smooth and shiny and she had to tear up her food with her fingers. She developed the flesh of a woman and breasts and everything else that grown women have, but never teeth.

At an early stage she started the habit of holding her hand in front of her mouth. Then she began to hold both hands in front of her face when she was with other people. After her breasts had developed her cheeks began to wrinkle, and although she was only just grown up she had already become shrunken and hollow about her eyes and mouth. But she still felt incessantly round her gums with her tongue: nothing is fixed for ever, and she had been specially anointed by the priest.

Ädla was also alive.

And Avar went on living. He was still lying in bed but he was alive. He was the only one who had been dying and had survived.

Though Könik thought that he continued to smell very strange.

The pustules had gone down and had left little black scabs; he wasn't hot any more and he was lying motionless, not shaking his head and flailing his arms, and his eyes were no longer wandering in all directions, he mostly just lay there looking at Ädla.

He didn't get up. Sometimes he would scratch his skin where a scab had come loose. It was self-evident that he ought to have died.

And Ädla thickened out. She had suddenly begun to eat everything she could find, more even than before, and it wasn't just her belly that swelled but also her cheeks and breasts and upper arms – yes, even her lips. When she took hold of Avar he could feel that her fingers had become softer, and he heaved a tormented sigh.

But she was moving more lightly than before. The heavier she got, the more lithe and supple her limbs became. No, it was as if her increasing weight was laid upon him, on his senses and on his soul, it lay across him and he was incapable of lifting himself up.

They never spoke about what had happened that time he had decided to teach her, not about that precise moment. Except that once Ädla said to Avar:

"I was filled with such a sense of wonder that I thought I would die."

That was the word she used. Wonder.


Those seven then. Borne and Bera and Ädla and Avar and Könik and Eira and Önde.

Önde sat with Avar for long periods at a time. Since that evening when Avar really should have died he felt he almost belonged to Ädla's and Avar's family. He told Avar that no one was dying any more, that life would go on. But Avar didn't seem

74

to care, he just moved one hand listlessly as if life were no more than a fly walking on him.

And it was Önde who told him what had happened to Könik's Eira. But even that lacked any meaning for Avar.

Yes, the paralysis really had held its hands over Eira and protected her. If she had been on her feet, if she had been her usual self, lively and unpredictable, then she would definitely have jumped right into the arms of death.

And Könik had looked after her as if she'd been a newborn babe, as if she'd been their first-born. He'd handled her as if she were a bowl he'd carved so fine that it was transparent. He'd been as chaste towards her as if she'd been his own daughter. And it was not impossible that despite her fear and terror she had actually enjoyed the paralysis itself.

Könik had begun to count and tell her how many days had passed without anyone dying. Two days, five days, twelve days, an unknown number of days.

Finally one evening he said: "Now I can't even remember any more when it was that I lost count."

Then, when they were lying there trying to sleep, she in her bed and he in his, in the dark, she said: "My feet are freezing."

Since she'd taken to her bed she hadn't said a single word about any individual part of her body. Könik was seized with an extraordinary feeling of passion when he heard her name her feet. He went over to her on his hands and knees and lifted up the fur cover to get to her feet, and he grasped hold of them as if they were pieces of bread that would put an end to his starvation, he took both her feet in his hands, he hugged them as if they were completely frozen and needed to be thawed. He did it gently and carefully, because it was impossible to know how frail and delicate they'd become from never being used, he was afraid the bones would break. But then he suddenly felt her wiggling her little toes in the palms of his hands, it was as if she wanted to tease and tickle him, and he really couldn't hold back a sudden laugh, or perhaps not a laugh but rather a kind of sigh of happiness. And then the other toes began to wake up one after the other and started bending and waggling and making fun of him.

When he had woken her feet he went on to the ankles, and now his hands were more sure and determined, and soon her ankle joints began to move. He could feel the sinews stretching and the heels moving up and down against his wrists as if she were walking in empty nothingness, as if she were coming to meet him without thinking what she was doing.

Then he curled his hands round her shins, thin and delicate as they were, and he pressed and kneaded them gently as if milking a young cow for the first time, and after a while the flesh became firmer and filled out the skin of her legs and began to tremble and quiver.

Now she spoke of her knees, and once more he was filled with that sudden incomprehensible feeling of passion.

And he lifted up the fur cover a little bit more and took her knees in his hands and stroked her kneecaps gently and tentatively, they were like polished stones in the palms of his hands, and he slipped his hands beneath her knees and lifted them slightly, very carefully, almost anxiously. There was a creaking in the joints like dry pieces of wood rubbing against one another, and he thought now I must have gone too far, her knees must have become permanently unusable, but when he let go she was able to keep her legs drawn up by her own effort.

Finally she spoke of her thighs and said: "It prickles and feels like ice inside my thighs."

And that was more than Könik could bear, hearing her speak of her own thighs by name, he became so aroused that he couldn't remain cautious and careful any longer. He bent down and crawled in completely under the fur cover, and began to warm her and rub her with the whole of his huge body. Huge, that is, in comparison with Eira's. At first she squealed and whimpered like a piglet caught under a flap in its pen, but said nothing, and after a while her whole body began to tremble, the

76

parts of her body began to wake up one after another without her saying a single word to them, and what was truly a thing to wonder at was how well they remembered what to do. She grasped Könik round the back of the neck with her hands and stroked him behind the ears with her fingertips where he was already wet with sweat. Her rib cage expanded and took his weight, she opened her mouth and sucked at his lower lip. Just as he had first awoken her feet, he now awoke Eira's whole and complete person – yes, it could almost be said that she was at that moment born anew.

That, or at least something roughly resembling that, was what Önde told Avar.

And it became known throughout the whole of Kadis – yes, Önde used the phrase "whole of Kadis" although it now meant so little – it became generally known that afterwards Eira was in the same condition as Ädla; it was probable that she had conceived at the same moment that – to use Könik's own words – he had caused her to be born anew. And Könik had talked about this in anguish and distress: Was it offending against the natural order of things to let oneself be born and fertilized at the same time, even in the same breath? Could that be right?

"Sometimes I think there's nothing that's natural and self-evident," said Avar. He caught his breath as he said it, it was probably the most dreadful blasphemy that had ever been expressed in Kadis.

Önde wanted to comfort him, because things were how they were with Ädla, and because he was lying where he lay, but above all because he had said something so abominable.

"If you were well," he said, "you wouldn't be tormented by such tribulations."

"I'm completely well," said Avar, "I can't remember being so well even in my youth."

"You'll soon be even better," said Önde, "that's only natural and self-evident, and then you'll be up and taking care of everything that's yours. The whole of Kadis will lie under your protection."

"Nothing is mine," said Avar. "I've never possessed anything, everything was a delusion of the devil, life itself is a delusion of the devil."

That too of course was a blasphemy, it was an insult to Kadis and to the prevailing order that even Önde couldn't brush off, and he got up and left. There was an unbearable smell of putrefaction and decay at Avar's bedside, and no one could endure sitting there for long.

Avar had forbidden Ädla to make a brightly blazing fire or to have the door open or to take down the pelts from the window openings, since he couldn't bear the light.

It was late afternoon now, and when Önde opened the door the sun shone right in on Avar. And Önde stood there for a moment forcing Avar to lie in the light, as if he wanted to say that there were some things that it wasn't worth trying to shut out and deny, such as light. It existed anyway, it was natural and self-evident.


When the first thaws came it began to smell sweet and peculiar and nauseating in Kadis. At first nobody noticed it, the smell crept up on them so slowly and gently that it seemed perfectly reasonable and normal and natural. It must have always smelled like that in the spring, anyway for as long as they'd had this Sickness – for that could hardly have been their first winter during the time of the Sickness and the rabbits. And if they thought about it carefully they might even be cheered and exhilarated by that damp vapour and sweetness that wafted about in the air between the houses.

But then Borne went to Umeå. He was away for three days. He just wanted to see whether Umeå was still there, whether the world still existed or whether it had perished. And when he

78

came back he told them that nothing had happened beyond Kadis. He was the type who never had anything to tell, someone else should have gone to Umeå. He had got himself a sack of salt in exchange for two sacks of rabbit pelts and a silver coin that Önde had provided him with.

Then he said: "But there's a dreadful stench here in Kadis."

And then they all noticed – all except Avar, of course – that there was an unbearable smell. They remembered too that the stench had been repulsive ever since the warm weather had begun, and that it had at times been so difficult to breathe that they had all lost the desire to eat and that they had often thought that the smell came from inside themselves. They had thought they were so unclean that they had avoided getting near each other.

So they set about looking for the source of all this stench. They hunted in the deserted houses and in the drying-sheds and storehouses.

And it's impossible to list all that they found.

There were hams and legs of lamb that were green and fell apart when they touched them, and buckets of fish that had fermented to a yellow froth, and calf heads with maggots crawling in and out of the eye sockets, and cheeses that were just rind covering rats which had died from overeating.

There was a dead cow lying in Thomas the butcher's cow-shed.

A pig had dug itself in under Evan's house, a subterranean passage, and he'd stuck fast.

Ädla found a rabbit underneath Avar: he had lain on it and crushed it to death.

They gathered up everything they found and threw it all in the river. They went down to the cross-currents right out at Calf Point and dropped it in the water, and the current immediately carried off the whole lot. They stayed there a while and watched it all float away and disappear, the calves' heads and bodies and legs of lamb and cheeses and the casks of fish, all

79

that was rotten and mouldy and fermented and decayed and all the carcasses, and from that day on they always referred to the river as she instead of it as before, and no one knew why that was. The river is still referred to as she today. She helped them get rid of all the stinking remains, she swept everything away.

They also took up the straw on the floors and beds. It was black and gave off appalling dust, not just the straw from the deserted houses but also that which they'd been lying on. There was plenty of dry unspoilt straw in the cow-shed lofts, and they even changed the straw under Avar. Borne lifted him up and held him while Ädla and Eira made a new bed for him. Avar pretended he was asleep.

It took them two days to clean up Kadis, and they worked without stopping, two sunny days with a steady wind from the coast. From time to time they paused and breathed in the new air which quite simply smelled of nothing. They liked it, but at the same time they had to admit inwardly to themselves that it lacked substance. Önde picked up a pig's skull and set it on a stake in front of the chapel. "We can't live here in Kadis," he said, "entirely without any smells at all."

They were all very tired afterwards but also strangely elated, it was as if they had been able for the first time in ages to satisfy a secret desire. They felt themselves liberated from something, though they weren't sure what it was.

And Könik rejoiced with the others. But he was still the sort of man he was, he could never be pleased and satisfied, for him there was no adequate or absolute cleanness. As soon as he was alone he pulled out his shirt so that he could stick his nose in and smell himself. He never managed to throw off the suspicion that there was something that was not as it should be, that deep within him there were still some dregs of putrefaction.

Then in the evening Avar said to Ädla: "I'll get up tomorrow and have a bath."

And when he woke in the morning that was the first and only thing he said: "Today's the day I'm going to get up and have a bath."

And Ädla knew that now, somehow, he was going to rid himself of whatever it was that had kept him held down in bed. Whatever had been too heavy for him to bear he had obviously decided to endure from now on, he was going to rise up and take the burden on his shoulders.

He was man enough after all.

So she trundled in the tub that they bathed in. It was Könik's father who had made it for Avar's father. They also used it for scalding pigs.

It was probably the fresh straw under him and the pure air that he'd all at once started to breathe that had made him realize the state he was in, he had become aware of his own smell and uncleanness.

And Ädla brought in water and filled the cauldron and lit the fire.

Then she went off towards the forest to collect juniper twigs. The ground behind Avar's sheep enclosure was covered in juniper bushes.

As she stood there breaking off twigs Önde came by, carrying a knife and an empty sack, on his way to cut birch bark.

"So you're going to brew some beer," he said.

"No," said Ädla, "not beer."

"You're going to chop up the juniper and mix it in with the mulch."

"No," said Ädla, "not that either."

"But you're collecting twigs," said Önde.

"Yes," said Ädla. "And I thought I'd get some bog-myrtle too if I could find any."

"I can get you some bog-myrtle down by the river," said Önde.

"Though I don't absolutely need bog-myrtle," said Ädla.

"I don't understand at all," said Önde.

She straightened up and turned her face towards him. She didn't really smile – no, she didn't go that far, but there was a kind of joy in her eyes.

"He's going to take a bath," she said.

"Avar's going to take a bath?" said Önde.

"Yes," said Ädla.

So Önde didn't go cutting birch bark, he turned round and went to Könik and told him that Avar was going to get up and have a bath.

Könik went in and told Eira.

Eira hurried off to Bera so that she could hear it too.

Then they went on together, Bera and Eira, to Borne. So all of Kadis knew that Avar was getting up now to wash himself.

Ädla had to heat four whole cauldrons before the tub was full enough. She had tied the twigs into a bundle that she dipped in the water as it was heating. It smelled like the forest in the fiercest heat of the sun or like beer fermenting, and Ädla thought: I only hope he doesn't change his mind. But she couldn't remember him ever, not even once, having changed his mind.

And just as she was pouring the last cauldron-full into the tub, Önde arrived with some bog-myrtle. Bera had tied it up with an osier twig that Borne had chewed soft for her. And Önde put the myrtle in Avar's bath water.

It was the first time in a long while that the fire had really lit up the house. The pelts were still hanging over the window openings, and Avar was lying with his face to the wall. But when

Ädla came and bent over him he turned round and looked at her.

There had been a blind man in Kadis called Ivald. Avar lay there and his eyes looked just as Ivald's used to. He seemed not to notice the light.

"Here's your bath water," said Ädla.

"Already?" said Avar. "Is it hot already?"

"The tub is steaming," said Ädla. "You be careful."

She hadn't seen his body since the time he'd decided to teach her, and she didn't want to see it. They had never given a thought to their bodies before.

"I'll be off," said Ädla. "I'm going to Eira's. Or to Bera. So I'll leave you alone to get up and have your bath just as you will."

When she said she would go away while he had his bath his head and shoulders jerked as if someone had hit him hard in the chest.

"And when you've bathed for as long as you want," said Ädla, "you can try coming out into the light and see how it feels to stand on your feet again."

Then she and Önde went off. "I've put some myrtle in for you," said Önde, and Ädla held her right hand under her belly as a support: she was not yet so swollen that it was noticeable, but if she stood upright for long or if she lifted or carried anything her belly felt terribly heavy, and it sometimes felt almost as if she would fall on her face.

She went to Eira's and helped her knead some dough. And Önde went to see Bera. He had promised to mend her roof; she'd got water in her cheese vat when the thaw came. And she had a goat with a wounded udder, the billy goat had made a deep cut in it. Someone was going to have to slaughter it for her.

So while Avar was taking his bath, everyone busied themselves with one thing or another. The animals had to be fed, those of the living and those of the dead, the midday meal had to be cooked, one of the cows that Thomas had left behind was about to calve – Borne was with her – and all the other cows would have to be milked before nightfall, all the cows in Kadis, and cream would have to be made from yesterday's milk, and butter churned. Önde looked after Evan's sow and piglet and fed them. And Könik was stripping and squaring pine logs, he had felled them himself on the common and was going to build himself something, though not even Eira knew what it was he had in mind. While they were busy doing what had to be done, while some of them were even running from one job to another so that nothing essential would be left undone, they were all thinking inwardly the whole time about the fact that Avar was taking a bath, that it was today he was getting up to have a bath.

Könik was also thinking: He knows how everything should be, he is the only one who can say what is necessary and fitting, and now he is still with us. He knows the order that has prevailed since time immemorial, he has the knowledge of right and wrong and what is proper, boundaries and laws and punishments and the rates of atonement, he can advise on rules and customs and mistakes. Now that Avar has finally risen from his bed and taken a bath we need no longer fear that Kadis will perish.

That, or something very much like it, was what Könik was thinking.

From time to time one of them would find a reason for going past Avar's house to see whether he might already be finished and standing in the doorway or sitting on the threshold.

And when all the cows had been milked and everything else done that was necessary and proper, they all gathered outside Avar's house. Ädla and Bera and Borne and Eira and Könik. And Önde.

They just stood there in devout silence, some of them remembering the time when the priest was still alive and they would stand waiting outside the chapel for some special and ceremonial event. And they were all thinking: We'll never forget this day, the day Avar had his bath.

"He'll be combing his hair, too," said Borne. "And trimming off the worst of his beard."

"He's never done things by halves," said Könik.

"No," said Önde. "What little he does, he does thoroughly."

"But perhaps he'd still like some help with something," said Eira.

"What Avar can't do himself," said Könik, "doesn't need doing."

"If he isn't man enough to bath himself," said Önde, "then it would have been better if he'd died."

"I'm freezing," said Ädla.

Önde went and fetched a cover from Evan's house and put it over her shoulders.

And they all felt that it was beginning to turn cold.

When the sun had gone down to the tops of the trees on the far side of the river, and when the whole of Kadis was glowing red from the last rays of sunlight, Borne said:

"He must have finished bathing by now."

"I expect he's gone back to bed again," said Eira. "He must have been tired after he'd had his bath, and fallen asleep again."

"He'll be too cold to go out," said Önde. "When you've been lying in bed for a long time, you're as cold as a newborn pig."

"Perhaps we should go in and light the fire for him," said Eira.

They stood in silence for a long time. Finally Könik said: "He can throw us out if he wants to, of course. If he as much as waggles his little finger we'll go again straight away."

So they went in to Avar's house; it was Ädla who opened the door and stood and held it for them. And Önde went across to the fireplace and blew life into the embers and lit a fire-stick so that they could see Avar.

He had his tunic on, he even had his sandals on his feet, and he was kneeling by the tub; he was kneeling exactly as they had been taught to kneel when praying to God. Eira and Könik used to kneel like that for a few minutes every evening. He had his head and neck and even a few inches of his shoulders in the water.

They saw immediately what had happened, and they all cried out – astonished or terrified or heart-rending cries – all except Ädla.

So there he was, and he'd drowned himself.

Könik dipped his hand in the tub and felt the water: it was ice-cold. And Borne held Avar round the waist and lifted him up. It must be his job now to take care of him, and he carried him the few steps over to the bed and laid him down.

They couldn't straighten him out, he lay like a baby just out of the womb, and they couldn't close his eyes. Önde held up the stick to cast light on him; his face was as white as snow, it must have been in the water almost the whole day. They had never seen a cleaner person.

The only one to say anything for a long time was Ädla. "It's my fault," she said.

He had taken hold of the bundles of myrtle twigs with both hands, the ones Önde had brought and put in the bath water, he was holding them to his chest the way women hold myrtle when they get married.

There was nothing anyone could do. They could do nothing for Avar and nothing for themselves.

What he looked like was the impossible concept of a wrinkled white-haired baby at its own wedding.

All they could do was to leave him where he lay. Ädla would sleep at Bera's that night.

When they were outside the door Önde said: "I would have had to straighten up and draw breath. What a man he was."

"Yes," said Borne. "He obviously did it himself."

That meant: He was a suicide, and they used to bury them out in the forest. It was Borne who would have to do it.

"No one does anything entirely by himself," said Könik,

86

"there's nothing that's so insignificant that you can do it solely by your own strength."

What that meant even he didn't know.

That evening Könik and Eira lay close together as was their custom. She lay with her back against his chest, huddled in the angle of his updrawn knees. Now and then Könik shook as if he was sobbing and weeping, and each time she patted him on the thigh without realizing she was doing it. And she said: "What is it, Könik?"

But it wasn't easy to understand what he was trying to say.

"Borne is going to bury him out in the forest," she thought she heard him say, "and I don't know whether that's right, it's impossible to know whether it's right. It was a terrible sickness that took his life, so he ought to be buried like everyone else. But he did it himself, so he ought to be buried out in the forest. When I saw Avar as he was just now, I was filled with shame. I was ashamed of what he had done with Ädla and I was ashamed that we in our innocence thought he was having a bath, and I'm ashamed that we don't know where we should bury him. And what is shameful is what is evil. We recognize evil through shame. We never needed to feel shame in Kadis before, we knew how to avoid shame because we knew what was forbidden. We had suffering, but no shame. When you feel shame the soul festers and becomes an abscess within the body. The soul should be like a warm breeze in the limbs. We should be at peace in our minds and bodies. Goodness is when everything is as it should be, goodness is what is right and proper. If everything is as it should be, then things are good and sensible. Common sense is the will of God, and here in Kadis we have always inherited common sense: fathers have passed it on to their sons. Everything was so simple, it was like a water-wheel that goes on and on as long as the water flows. There was a sure way of living and everything seemed to have its own reason. But now it's

87

impossible to know what's right. Kadis has broken apart."

It's not certain that he said exactly that, but what she heard was something like that. Perhaps it was only here and now that everything really began. She went on patting him on the thigh until he fell asleep.

And now Evan's sow had farrowed. In fact she was nobody's sow any more, and it was Önde who looked after her. It took her, or more accurately her and Önde, a whole day and a whole night to give birth to this one piglet.

The sow was five feet long and she was called Pila. She had black forequarters and white hindquarters, and Önde thought she'd had five litters before. She used to go into the forest with Evan and help him look for birds' nests: she would stand under a tree and squeal. Her legs were as long as a sheep's, and she had twelve teats.

Önde had been waiting for her to farrow for a long time. She was so heavy that she mostly just stood in her sty swaying from side to side, and despite the fact that her legs were so long her belly hung down to the ground.

Önde happened to be there the morning she lay down to farrow, and he thought: I'll stay here and save half of them. She can eat the other half, we don't need so many pigs here in Kadis any more.

Sows usually farrow with incredible ease, they just lie down and the piglets pop out in a steady stream. Some sows seem to lie there thinking of something else entirely, they don't seem to notice what's happening to them; many sows even fall asleep while they're farrowing.

But things were very different for Pila. She lay there twisting and turning this way and that, and squealing and whimpering so pitifully that Önde's eyes filled with tears as he listened to her.

Finally he decided that he really must help her. And so he

set one foot on her head to hold her still, and pressed firmly with the other foot on her belly. He put his foot against her lowest rib and pushed with all his might.

She screamed in mortal anguish, but at the same time she opened up and something began to squeeze out of her. When Önde looked more closely he saw that it was a pig's foot, an extraordinarily large foot for an unborn piglet, a black foot.

And he thought to himself: Now it's moving, now she'll manage it. And he turned the sow over and sat on her.

But for ages it seemed as if she wasn't going to give birth to more than this one foot. She got up and stood for a while swaying unsteadily to and fro and then flopped flat down again on her left side and went straight to sleep.

So passed the whole afternoon and evening and night. Önde fetched some straw and made himself a bed next to the sty. Now and again she got up as if she wanted to try to flee from this dreadful business of giving birth, and sometimes she whimpered like an abandoned baby, but mostly she just slept, and that pig's foot hung out of her, heavy and unmoving.

But just before dawn her whole body began to shake, it looked as if some terrible subterranean power was making the earth shudder beneath her, and her flesh wobbled as if it had been cooked and just lifted out of the stew-pot. And she was racked by cramps that made her kick her legs and bang her head as if she was trying to beat and pound herself to death.

Yes, it was more than Önde could bear to watch.

And he climbed in with her and crouched down in front of her and tried to take her tormented head on his lap. Her whole snout was covered in froth. "You wretched, helpless and confounded pig. You poor lost soul," he said.

And when she saw him she suddenly became quite calm again, but it was a deceptive calm. All the strength that she had just been using against herself in cramps and tremors was now gathered up and turned against Önde: she sprang up and cast herself upon him with a monstrous roar. She thought it was he who had caused her this grim suffering, this injustice. She snapped at his neck and face and she hit out at his arms with her forelegs, she was in a trance-like state of rage and wanted to kill him. Önde was ready for anything – he always was – he braced himself to jump up and meet her. But it was slippery in the sty from her excrement and the crushed straw: his feet slid away from him and he fell flat on his back. The sow missed his neck and face with her teeth, and flew over him and landed with her stomach on his chest. Önde could feel the pig's foot which she had managed to give birth to swinging and banging against the lower part of his leg. He heaved her off, jumped up quickly and threw himself at her, got on her back, forced his arms under her and clasped his hands together so that his fingers couldn't be pulled apart. Two of her teats got caught between his knuckles and her roaring turned into a high drawn-out scream, she twisted and wriggled and stamped her feet in her efforts to free herself, but he didn't let go and he was terribly strong – he pushed and wrestled and renewed his attempt to hold her down and subdue her, he sat upon her with such force that a normal pig would have spewed up its guts. And so they went on wrestling till daybreak.

But then the sow was finally conquered, she fell heavily on her side and closed her eyes as if she were dead, she was gasping for breath most horribly but not grunting or whimpering, she was completely silent – and when Önde turned his head to see whether anything had happened he noticed that another foot had squeezed out and that was also black.

Önde too was rather limp and breathless, but he realized the moment had come when he really could help her, so he got on his knees behind her and grasped one foot in each hand – they were slimy and slippery and he had to dry his palms on his tunic again and again – and he pulled and heaved and tugged, slowly and carefully so as not to hurt her unnecessarily, and bit by bit the piglet came out – Önde saw at once that it had been the wrong way round in her womb – hind legs first and thighs and belly, it was a boar, and chest and neck and finally head and snout – and it was half black and half white.

The sow gave a long deep sigh of relief, but she was bleeding dreadfully. The piglet had torn her apart, the blood was flowing as if she had been slaughtered instead of delivered. Önde ran to Evan's house and fetched some clothes that were lying there and that obviously nobody would need any more and tore them into long strips, and he bandaged up the' sow, he lay down behind her and wrapped and tied and knotted as best he could, and she lay absolutely still and let him do it – yes, she even drew up her legs to her belly to make it easier for him to pull the strips round over her back.

Then Önde lifted the piglet over to her and it began to suck straight away. Finally he went home to sleep. Such a farrowing, even he could see, would never have taken place in Kadis as it once was. It had elements of fable and absurd fiction about it that offended all too grossly against the accepted order. The old men would have come to slaughter the sow as soon as the piglet's first, unbelievable foot had squeezed out of her. He was pleased that he had been able to deliver her.

He slept for the rest of that day and the whole of the night, so thoroughly had the sow exhausted his strength.

And he continued to look after Pila and the piglet, he changed her bandages and made sure that the torn flesh and skin were healed, and he brought her food and played with the piglet and nursed him and watched over him. He was incredibly greedy – if the sow and Önde hadn't curbed him and hit him on the snout he would have swallowed her teats as well.


But then it was arranged that Könik and Eira would have him. They hadn't kept pigs before, Könik had always got meat by barter from Evan. He built himself a little pig-sty behind his carpenter's shop, and he made an opening in the wall and a pen on the outside too so that the piglet himself could choose whether to be outside or inside.

And Önde was there explaining to Könik how a pig liked its surroundings to be, and he spoke to Eira about his food – they shouldn't imagine that keeping pigs was just a kind of pastime. It wasn't at all easy for Önde to give up the pig; it sometimes almost felt as if it was his own flesh and blood.

When Könik brought the pig home he didn't carry him in his arms the way people usually did with piglets, he had him in a barrow that he was pushing in front of him – he was already too heavy to be carried. Eira hadn't seen him before.

"Is that the little piglet?" she asked.

"The very same," said Könik.

"He's hideous," said Eira. "He doesn't look like a pig."

"When he was first born," said Könik, "he most resembled a dog. And he barked. But he looks more and more like a pig with every day that passes."

"A pig should look like a pig and not like anything else," said Eira.

Könik put down the shafts of the barrow and straightened up. The pig was sitting exactly like a dog. This was the first time he'd been outside his sty and he was turning his head inquisitively this way and that. His eyes were surprisingly large and black.

"We know so awfully little," said Könik. "We imagine we understand everything. We think we can distinguish between right and wrong simply with our eyes."

"Yes," said Eira. "That's true."

"Whereas in fact," Könik went on, "we know nothing about the true nature of the world."

So they put him into the pig-sty. Eira had some sour milk and she'd boiled turnips and pea pods for him and they gave him an armful of straw so that he could make himself a bed.

And Könik had to take away the top bar of the pen so that Eira could come and scratch him and talk to him. She got used to him looking as he did, and he also became more and more

93

pig-like and less dog-like, he stopped barking and now just grunted and snorted like an ordinary pig. He ate everything she gave him and soon he was as tall as Eira when he stood on his hind legs and put his forefeet on the bars of the pen.

And when Könik very tentatively first proposed a time far in the future when it might possibly be right to slaughter the pig, Eira immediately started talking about something else – about the salmon Önde had come over with and about going to see how Ädla was, and about Borne having killed the goat for Bera that the billy goat had injured, and about Borne trying to make a rucksack for Bera from the skin.

Has it been mentioned that the pig had a name? It was Önde who found a name for him: he was called Blasius.

And so inheritances were redistributed in Kadis. It happened almost unnoticed, without anyone deciding that it should be done, without heirs being sure of their rights, without rule or order – there were no rules. It was a faltering and uncertain and dubious distribution of inheritance, based on guesswork and indistinct memory and unfounded assertions; it was impossible to carry out but also impossible to avoid.

The only one who pretended to be certain that property limits and boundary lines and owners' marks still had a meaning was Önde. And that it was still possible to own things at all.

Önde was two deep notches with a shallow cut across them. Borne was a simple square. Könik was a droplet, or, if the sign were viewed from the opposite end, a candle flame. He was the only one who could cut curved lines with a knife.

There were no signs for the women.

Önde carved his notches on Thomas' house and Jalte's and Tvare's and Uno's. "Someone has to take pity on the houses," he said. "They can't just be left to their fate, without a master." And when Könik asked why it had to be specifically his mark that was carved on the walls, he always had an answer: they had been distant relatives, it had been uttered on a deathbed, he had claims for debts from the deceased.

Before the Sickness came Önde had owned nothing but his house and a cow. And that beard comb that might be silver.

Borne collected things and carried them home to his own house. But he did it without plan or calculation, as if absent-mindedly. He would see something lying on the ground or leaning against a tree and he would pick it up and take it. And so a huge pile of rakes and spades and axes and scythes and fish-spears and pots and sledges and all manner of inherited property grew up outside his house. Ädla helped herself to things too, mostly pelts and cloth and yarn that nobody had yet made anything from, and unspun wool.

But Bera took nothing. Anyone who has goats, goats that give milk and billy goats that eat at your table and kids that sit on your lap and sleep in your bed, doesn't need anything else.

Where did it begin and where would it end, this distribution of inheritance?

One afternoon Önde came to Könik with all Yvar's tools. He was carrying them on Jalte's cart that was now his. Pliers and hammers and files and anvils and everything that Yvar had had in his smithy.

"You might as well," said Önde.

"I don't know," said Könik.

"You may have some use for them," said Önde.

"They're really still Yvar's," said Könik.

And then the worry kept him awake the whole night.

Önde came by from time to time carrying this, that or the other that he thought should rightfully be Könik's: drills and material for sledge runners and tubs and spits and axes – yes, anything and everything. He wanted Könik to benefit from the distribution of inheritance. And every time Könik lost sleep over it.

Önde would also sometimes dig up the dead. He would suddenly remember that there was a ring left on a finger in the hurry or a chain around a neck or a clasp on a blouse. He might dig in several different places before he found what he was looking for, he didn't always understand the markers Könik had put up and he didn't want to ask. He thought no one knew what he was doing. Or he pretended to think that no one knew. And they pretended that they didn't know.

If there had been any surviving woman to inherit, Borne

would have taken her hand and she would have had to go with him.

Late one evening as Könik was passing Tvare's cow-shed he noticed that the door wasn't bolted on the outside. So he went and peeped in. And there was Borne with Tvare's heifer – another inheritance appropriated. He was holding up her tail with his right hand and doing with her what he should have been doing with a woman if he'd had one. To get to the heifer and make use of her like that he had climbed up on the milk pail. She was a fine and long-legged heifer. Könik had made that milk pail for Tvare several years before. The next day Könik went back and took the pail: he felt he had a greater right to it than Borne, and he couldn't bear to see a pail he had made with his own hands so degraded and defiled.

One day Önde came by with a necklace for Eira. It was made of silver. He put it over her head and round her neck. "I want you to have it," he said, "I've thought for a long time that this necklace is as if made for you."

When Könik came home he said: "Where did you get that necklace?"

"I got it from Önde."

"You've got it from Jalte's wife Åsa," said Könik, "I recognize it very well – Åsa had it round her neck when I laid her in her coffin."

Eira ripped off the necklace and went outside and vomited.

But afterwards, when she had completely finished retching, she went down to the river and washed the necklace clean. She held it in the flowing water till her hand went numb and felt as if it were dead. And after that she had the necklace constantly round her neck.

But Könik burned the milk pail.

Yes, where did it begin and where did it end, this distribution of inheritance? Könik seemed to be the only one who really noticed, or even noticed at all, that it was going on.

Long ago, before this story began, when they had only recently become man and wife, Könik used to carry Eira on his shoulders; she had ridden on his shoulders like a little child and pressed her groin against the back of his neck. Now he had completely forgotten that they had been able to run about in so trusting and childlike a manner on the paths of Kadis.

He had started to chew strips of birch bark, it made him feel calmer for a while. But he got ulcers on his gums and lips. And the fresh juice from the birch bark filled his mouth, but that was all; it didn't penetrate to his senses where his anxiety and confusion were growing relentlessly.

It was a greater help if he cut and sawed wood and made things. But when he sat down to rest for a while, when tiredness began to make his shoulders ache, he would let his eyes look back at what his hands had just done, and then that gnawing anxiety would come over him again and his eyes would have no real pleasure.

He built something that no one before him had made in Kadis: a room. A room that would belong to the house. He fixed it to the old corner joints and he laid the roof beams so that the old roof would continue into the new. The room would be almost as big as the house, and he would make benches along the walls, benches that were wide enough for someone to sleep on if they wanted to. Perhaps one day a stranger would come who would need to sleep in his house. He would make an opening in the roof and build a fireplace so that they could heat the room in winter; and he and Eira were already talking about the house and the room and what they would be able to do in the room in the future that they now did in the house.

Könik was thinking of the child that Eira was carrying; the child would have both a house and a room.

And in the evenings he sat carving a devil – he'd saved a tree trunk for it that was five feet tall and that he could hardly get his arms round. It was the priest who'd suggested it when Könik had finished that big cross in the chapel: "We need saints too, a long row of saints, and a devil that I can point to when I'm teaching the people."

Könik knew all too little about saints, he knew only a few by name, but the priest had described the devil to him – yes, he had even drawn him on a piece of birch bark. He would really have liked to have him painted on the wall, but there was nobody who could paint even the simplest flourish or picture or who knew how to grind or mix colours.

Of course the priest was dead now, but Könik still hoped that a new priest would come one day. He tried to think forward to that uncertain future when the devil would be of use after all.

He had a high pointed hat, hair on his body and an unkempt beard and long tail with a tuft, little horns on his knees and elbows, and his tongue protruded from his mouth and had a forked tip. His feet were goat's hooves and his hands would be shaggy with claws like a lynx.

And as Könik sat and carved him and turned him in his hands and polished him and stroked him with his fingertips, as he strove to make him as perfect as it was in his power to do, he was filled with affection for him, he couldn't help beginning to fall in love with this devil.

The face was the hardest. He'd understood that it ought to radiate both cruelty and cunning, that the mouth and the nostrils should be terrifyingly big and that the eyes should be open wide like a ravenous beast of prey.

But however he carved and cut and filed, however much he

99

moved wrinkles and lines and however he distorted the features, the face didn't go the way it should. Beneath the surface, beneath the rings in the wood and the streaks of the sap, it retained a basic element of goodness. Yes, and what was worse, the devil's face resembled Önde's.

And Eira said: "Why does he look like Önde?"

"He doesn't look like Önde," said Könik.

"The cheekbones and lower jaw and forehead," said Eira, "it's all like Önde. Even that hat on his head."

"Everyone has a jaw and cheekbones and a forehead," said Könik.

"So the devil is a person," said Eira. "You know for certain that he's a man, do you?"

"He's supposed to be able to sneak up on us," said Könik. "So he has to look like a human being. He's supposed to deceive us. He's supposed to be able to befriend us. And women are supposed to be able to fall in love with him."

"I'd never be able to love that wooden goat," said Eira.

"Not you," said Könik. "You can love only me. But ordinary women."

"Yes, of course," said Eira.

"And if you look closely," said Könik, "you'll see he has a tail and goat's hooves and claws like a cat's and horns in various places."

"Yes," said Eira. "But by then it might be too late."

They stood in silence for a moment admiring the creature Könik had made.

"I don't know anyone else who could carve a devil like this," said Könik.

And that was undeniably right. There was a gentle and almost seductive but nevertheless frightening beauty in Könik's devil. The grain in the wood imbued his skin with shadow and light, his hair curled at the temples, the outline of his manhood showed beneath his tunic and his eyes were the knots where two branches had grown, so they even had pupils.

"But I still don't understand why he should look like Önde," said Eira.

So now Könik had to admit what the problem was.

"I can't manage it," he said. "I've really tried to file off everything that might look like Önde. But it's been wasted effort."

"It must be devil's timber," said Eira.

"Yes," said Könik.

He suddenly sounded so miserable that Eira had to reach up and stroke his lower lip with her forefinger. They were standing on the floor in front of the devil. Whenever Könik was on the point of despairing it always seemed as if there wasn't enough air for his voice, it sounded like the whimpering of a puppy.

And Eira wished that she could have understood better what he was saying.

His tools no longer obeyed him, his chisels and knives were no longer aware of what was right and wrong, they made grooves and lines and smooth surfaces where he hadn't intended at all. Or maybe it was his hand that had lost its ability to judge and steer: sometimes he could just stand and watch his hand moving this way and that and hammering and carving and cutting as if it were a separate living entity, and had completely lost its sensitivity and humility. His hand had never behaved like that in the time when everything was as it should be in Kadis.

And the timber had become unpredictable and perverse, he could no longer rely on it, it twisted and bowed and shrank and swelled in all directions without any reason, it would no longer comply with his will at all. One day a piece of wood could be perfectly free of knots and the next day completely covered and riddled with rock-hard black knots. In the moment it took him to change a knife for a chisel or just to blink, the most wonderful piece of timber, the smoothest piece of wood, could turn into the most impossible piece of cross-grain. Things had never been like that before with timber in Kadis.

It was the same with the light, it deceived him all the time, both the daylight and the light from the tar-stick. It cast shadows where there should be no shadows, and it shimmered and shone where there ought to be only darkness and obscurity. And sometimes it just lay like grey dust or dirt over everything he had gone to so much trouble to make. The old light in Kadis had never been like that.

Not to mention his own eyes. They didn't see at all what he wanted to see, they projected distorted and false images to him, evil where they should rightly see goodness, and joy where they should see sorrow – yes, they had even seen a saint in this devil. His eyes now misunderstood most of what came into their vision. His eyes had understood everything in Kadis before.

It was probably the same now for all of them who had managed to survive. They had seen this creature that he had made, and Bera had said that that was what Avar would have looked like if he had put on a goatskin. Borne thought it looked rather like a poor wretch he had had to hang a few years ago, and Ädla had just said a few words about it resembling more or less anyone at all. Önde had said that yes indeed we might all be a bit like that, no living creature can fail to recognize himself in it.

But in times gone by, when everything was as it should be, every single person in Kadis would have said straight away: "Yes, of course, it's quite obvious: it's the devil."

That was probably not word for word what Könik said, but it was what Eira afterwards thought she could remember. She took his hand and pressed it and rubbed it against her forehead, as if to warm the hand he'd talked about or to impress on her own head what he had tried to explain to her.

"This is really dreadful, you must do something about it," she said.

"Yes. I'll have to do something about it."

"This can't carry on for all eternity," said Eira.

If he'd asked her what it was that couldn't go on for all eternity, she wouldn't have had any answer.

"I'll go to Umeå," said Könik. "Perhaps there'll be some kind of help there. There's salt and forging iron and knowledge in Umeå. So you can never tell."

"Yes," she said. "Do that. Go to Umeå."

She couldn't for the life of her understand why he should want to go to Umeå.

"And I can see rabbits everywhere," said Könik.

"Yes," she said. "There are rabbits everywhere."

"If only I knew," he said, "what it is that I should ask for or look for."

He was glad that he'd finally plucked up courage to tell her about Umeå, that he was going to leave her alone for a few days. He suddenly felt warm with irresolute decisiveness.

"But Önde isn't a devil," she said.

"No," said Könik, "Önde is goodness itself. If I were to attempt to carve those saints, they'd all end up looking like Önde. I don't know any better person than him."

He was silent for a moment. And then he added: "But that doesn't prevent him also being a devil."


So he went to Umeå.

And he asked everyone he met about one thing and another, to what extent this sickness that was called the Great Sickness was over and done with in the town, whether they still knew – or perhaps had had to learn again – what was right and proper, whether there were priests still alive in Umeå, whether anyone knew what should be done about children that men had fathered on their daughters, and how they should proceed with property that nobody owned, such as fields and houses and buried leather bags of gold coins and pieces of silver. In other words, whether it was known how law and order could be re-established to make everything as it should be, how everything that had been wiped out could be resurrected.

But they were uncommunicative in Umeå.

It was probable that they simply didn't understand gloomy Könik and his unfathomable quest.

"Ask that sort of thing up in the forests," someone said. "Here on the coast everything has been right and proper since time immemorial."

"We usually whip people who ask those sorts of questions," said another.

But one person said that yes indeed, the Sickness was over. And they had buried their dead.

And he repeated it: "We have buried our dead."

"We've buried them too," said Könik. "And the one who got his daughter with child we've buried out in the forest."

And someone said: "Well, that's all right, then."

"There are six of us left alive," said Könik. "In the whole of Kadis there are just six, and that's all of us."

"Well, you'll have to get going and multiply," said the man who'd talked of whipping. "If you still know how to go about it up there in the forests."

And the one who had admitted that the Sickness had gone asked: "But have you got food?"

"Yes," said Könik. "We've got enough food to feed the whole of Umeå."

"Well, that's all right, then," said the one who obviously always said that.

"But then there's the question of property and priests and law and order," said the one who'd talked about everything down at the coast being right and proper since time immemorial.

"Yes," said Könik. "Someone must come to Kadis and help us."

The people of Umeå were silent for a while. But then the one who'd talked about whipping, the one who thought they should multiply in Kadis, said – and he said it sharply so that no one would think it worthwhile saying anything more – "Out here on the coast we look after ourselves."

So Könik set off for home.

But when he came to the hillock by the river that they called the Hill he saw that they'd hanged a man. It looked as if it had only just taken place because a crowd of people was still standing around.

Könik sat down on a rock. It was a man of his own age or perhaps a bit older. When he swung round in the wind you could see that his hair was thin at the back, he looked so ordinary that Könik almost felt he recognized him. It was gruesome, but nevertheless it was as it should be.

There was a man standing just behind Könik chewing a strip of birch bark. He had large ulcers on his lips. Könik turned and asked him about the man they'd hanged.

"The law convicted him," the man said.

"Yes. The law convicted him."

Those were the finest words Könik had heard for a long time, he was amazed at himself when he realized how beautiful he thought they sounded: "The law convicted him."

Then he asked why the law had convicted him.

Well, what had happened was that there was a shortage of children. In many places there were no children at all, the children had been wiped out by that Great Sickness that there'd been everywhere. And many people were on their own now, or for one reason or another couldn't have more children. Children weren't something that grew out of the ground, either they came into the world or they didn't. So there were some people in these difficult times who stole themselves a child where they could: usually it was babies and they re-christened them and made them their own. In other places children had simply become wares to be traded, people stole and sold and bought children as if they were sacks of salt or beaver pelts. Sometimes people who didn't need a child would even abduct one dishonestly just because others were doing it. It had become a kind of sickness, this thing about children. The man they'd hanged came from Hiske, he was a widower and had lost all eight of his children. He had stolen a newborn child in Lövön.

"Though they could have let him go," said the man chewing birch bark. "The child was recovered and he was dreadfully full of remorse, and he'd even arranged for the child to inherit all he possessed. It was really only a matter of chance that he'd gone to Lövön and stolen a child. He'd said himself: 'I did it in a kind of trance.'"

But then Könik got up from the rock he'd been sitting on, and now he spoke so loud, but at the same time so falteringly and uncertainly, that it was almost impossible to understand what he was saying:

"Anyone who so much as offers a little finger to chance or trance has only himself to blame. You have to fight against chance and eradicate it if you can, and you have to wake and rise up from trance. This man who had stolen a child by accident in Lövön, he should be grateful there was a law and a system and a precedent to take charge of him, that there was a procedure for his particular case. He ought to know, the hanged man, that is, that there were people who were forced to live without order or meaning, and just had to make do with how things happened to be."

Like now in Kadis.

No, what had occurred here was just as simple and good as the grass growing and God letting the dead rise up on the appointed day, it was quite simply necessary. He said the word "necessary" with some difficulty, it was so big that there was hardly room for it in his mouth. What he would have liked to say about the word necessary was that it was weightier and more beautiful than anything else. "I can never," said Könik, "carve anything with my knife or chisel so perfect as the concept of necessity. Man cannot live without the concept of necessity. I'm a carpenter," he explained, "and I also carve pictures. It's necessary for causes to be followed by their effects, for the one to happen first and the other second and for people to take it for granted – yes, for us just to conform and go on without even looking for what's necessary and proper, for us to accept things as if they were the bread and wine of God. We can't live as if in a story, where anything at all can happen, higgledy-piggledy and without any order or meaning." That was all he wanted to say.

The man chewing birch bark thought he understood that that was what Könik meant.

But before he'd thought out what he could reply – and he probably ought to say something, since he'd sort of taken on responsibility for the hanged man – Könik had gone. He had to get back home to Kadis.


He was only away two days. When he returned, he'd just sat down and drunk a bowl of soup when Bera and Borne and Ädla and Önde came over: they knew that he'd come back from Umeå.

So Könik talked about what he had heard.

And when he spoke about people stealing children, all sorts of children but especially sons – people did it to replace children they'd lost – yes, they even stole them to sell as if they were salt or silver – when he said that, Ädla and Eira put their hands over their bellies as if already to start watching over their children and protecting them. Even Bera took her hands away from her face and put them over an imagined child – a child that she'd never even dreamed of before but which now she could suddenly visualize quite clearly.

And Könik mentioned that many of the men in Umeå were now wearing something called trousers, and their tunics were cut off at the hips. And that the law convicted people who stole children. He'd also thought that if he described the trousers very precisely to Eira she'd easily be able to make some for him. They could be either of leather or of cloth.

Then they had a long and thorough discussion about trousers, about how much cloth or leather would be needed and where the seams should be and how they should be made so that you could take them off, and whether they could be the same at the front and the back – as if these trousers were the one thing they had really lacked. They had all in various ways been tormented by a vague feeling that Kadis was imperfect now. It was a relief for them to find a word and an object that at least for the time being seemed to represent the thing they had lacked.

After Eira had sewn some trousers for Könik, she helped Ädla to make the ones Önde was going to wear. And Bera and Ädla made Borne's – his were made of rabbit skins and had a pouch at the side where he could keep a knife or his cupping iron: he was the only one now in Kadis who knew how to open veins. Or he could quite simply put his hand in the pouch if it was cold. Twenty skins went to make up Borne's trousers, he had such immense thighs.

The rabbits in Kadis were not really so very numerous, but they were everywhere. Some were in the houses, both the inhabited and the deserted ones, and many were living in the straw of the beds. Those rabbits had names and were recognizable – yes, they even had personal histories. There was always some feature to identify a particular rabbit: its ear-tufts, a black cross on its back, an injured leg or some other mark that made them individuals or even poor wretches.

But there were also the nameless ones, the ones that were here, there and everywhere and that didn't lead lives that could be described. Sometimes they were in the forest and sometimes in Kadis itself; they were as shy as hares and ran much faster and in a more terrified way than the familiar rabbits with names. They had become wild but they still harboured a dreadful anxiety since their time with humans, nothing was laid down and natural for them any more, they dug their holes all over the place.

Könik couldn't stand the wild rabbits.

He didn't talk to Eira about it. But if he had tried, he would have said that they were riotous and godless, that they were also perhaps in some inexplicable way dangerous. Who could say for certain that rabbits would never grow fangs and claws? He'd heard the wild rabbits hissing like lynxes; they'd probably start howling like wolves next.

On one occasion Önde said: "It's strange, when I was a child there were no rabbits in Kadis."

"No, that's true," said Borne. "I hadn't thought of that before. But it's right: there wasn't a single rabbit."

"If there had been rabbits," said Önde, "we wouldn't have forgotten about it."

"We would have hunted them," said Borne. "And made cages for them and collected birch twigs for them in the forest."

"And we would have tried baby rabbits as bait down at the river," said Önde.

"It's strange," said Borne. "But there must have always been rabbits in the forest, I suppose."

"Yes," said Önde. "And some made their way to Kadis and became tame."

"Though it's odd," said Borne, "that we can't remember when it happened."

But then Könik shouted at them: "It was Jasper of course who came back with that doe rabbit! He'd been to Nordingrå. He was looking for a woman. And you, Önde, made a hat from the fur."

He hadn't got that hat any longer. He'd blocked up a chink in the wall with it and the rats had eaten it.

"Yes, of course," said Önde.

"Yes," said Borne, "that's what happened."

And they fell silent, they looked down at the ground as if Könik had reminded them of something extraordinarily depressing or as if they were ashamed of having forgotten Jasper and the old doe rabbit – yes, as if they'd committed a grave sin in allowing themselves to forget almost everything.

"I wonder when it can have been," Borne said at last.

"It was the same year that father died," said Önde.

"It was the same year that everyone started dying," said Könik.

"It's a long time ago," said Borne.

"It's ages," said Önde.

And now Könik would have liked to tell them how long a time had passed since Jasper came home from Nordingrå with the rabbit. He wished he could have said how many years it was and how many weeks and days it was and how many new moons there'd been. But he couldn't.

He only knew that it was a terribly long time ago.

"No," he said, "it can't really be such a dreadfully long time ago."

So now they set about counting and calculating the time that had passed. They tried to arrange the past in years and days and seasons, they helped one another to remember so that some sort of chain of events might emerge. They explored the difference between first and next, and between latest and earliest and beginning and end. In the first instance they endeavoured to make hooks and loops of various particular happenings and events on which to fix or hang the rest of the time that had passed.

A cow is with calf for 290 days. The priest was one of the first to die. When the ice on the river has melted, summer is on its way. Once it had snowed on the cloudberries. A woman is pregnant for 270 days. Thomas the butcher said just before he died that he was forty. Some rabbits seem to give birth the very day they've been covered. Avar was the last to die. No, he didn't die. On the first hot spring day of one unknown year Yvar's cow got anthrax and Thomas had to slaughter her, so Thomas was alive then. Jalte had five children and they all died the same day, and that was before Avar said that the chapel was his. When Olavus the trader came Jalte was still alive, because he had shown him the way. No, Jalte was dead then, Olavus found the way himself. And now it's autumn. It's the autumn when Ädla and Eira are going to give birth. We mustn't forget that. And soon it'll be winter. It's the winter when we'll have to help one another mend the roof that collapsed on Yvar's smithy. We can't manage without a smithy and we're handy fellows, all three of us. "At least, you and I are, Könik," said Önde.

That's how it was with time, the years and days that had passed and their actual number – they had made themselves uncountable by merging into one another and making themselves unrecognizable and all alike. One moment had been over almost as soon as it had started, and another had lasted as long as any of them could remember. One day something was there and the next day it wasn't or hadn't even started to be. Sometimes a person was alive and sometimes dead, one instant it was summer, the next it was winter. Mostly they'd gone around looking down at the ground, but if they'd looked up it had sometimes been cloudy and sometimes sunny, sometimes dark and sometimes light. Most things were gone and some things were still left.

So they gave up, Önde and Könik and Borne, as if this business of the passage and order of time had no real significance, or as if they feared that time might stop if they actually succeeded in measuring it.

It was impossible to know how long it was since that day when Jasper had come home from Nordingrå.

And Könik of course was disconsolate. Time was as problematical as everything else.

"But the rabbits are a curse," said Borne.

"Yes," said Önde. "They eat the cabbages. And the bark on the lilac trees."

Önde had two lilac trees by his house. It was Cecilia who had planted them while she was with him. When they were in bloom he would never leave home, he just sat looking at the blossoms. They were blue.

"And they dig burrows," said Borne. "Under the houses and everywhere."

"I was walking through the grass in front of Bera's house,"

said Könik. "I thought I was going to fall down into hell. But it was only a hole the rabbits had dug."

"They're like vermin," said Önde.

"We should exterminate them," said Borne.

"It wouldn't work," said Könik. "As you're killing one, another would be giving birth to ten new ones."

"But even so," said Borne. "We should teach them a lesson. One they'd understand."

They sat in silence and thought for a while. Then Könik said: "But somehow they're so innocent, and their meat has hardly any taste."

Right at that moment a big fat old rabbit came hopping up to them, nuzzling at Borne's rabbitskin trousers and Önde's thong sandals. Önde put his hand down and lifted it up and stroked its back and bent forward and rubbed his face against its fur. It was one of the white ones that didn't even have black tufts on its ears, and Önde tickled it with his finger between its forelegs. Then suddenly he grabbed hold of it over its eyes and around its muzzle, pulled with a jerk and broke its neck.

And that was like a signal for Könik and Borne. They too had to do something about the rabbits. Önde set to with his teeth on the neck of the old rabbit and bit round the skin so that he could pull its head completely off, and Könik and Borne started running and hunting down all the rabbits they could see. Könik was faster than the heavier Borne, he could even catch up with rabbits that were fleeing towards the forest, and they seized doe rabbits and young rabbits that had crept under cover everywhere, beneath steps and behind woodpiles and in last year's hay and under upturned wooden tubs. They wrung their necks or grabbed them by the hind legs and dashed them against a wall or a rock. And they went into the deserted houses and rummaged for rabbits in wood-bins and food cupboards and clothes boxes. Borne even found a buck rabbit that had made its home in Gote's meat pan: he lay there trembling as if he'd been expecting to be put over the fire. When their hands got too

113

bloody to get a good grip they dried them off on the grass. They were wet with sweat, especially Könik; he wasn't even really thinking properly about what he was doing, he was rushing around as if in a trance. They were shouting to one another eagerly and excitedly and gasping for breath and even chuckling and laughing, and when one of them caught a particularly big or fine or strangely coloured or patterned rabbit he would hold it up by the hind legs and yell with delight and amazement so that the other two hunters could also see it before he slammed it against the wall. No, Könik wasn't really thinking about what he was doing, all he wanted was to liberate Kadis, at least from the rabbits, and now he could use his own hands to bring about some kind of purge and justice and restitution. It was the unruly confusion of existence that he was beating to death time after time against logs and sharp rocks. The rabbits might not be responsible for the disintegration and disorder, but they represented it, and Könik was the nimblest and most energetic of the three men, he ran to and fro so fast that his feet often slipped from under him on the grass and he fell headlong. The rabbits used the same trick as hares when they have a dog or wolf after them: they never ran straight but only by twists and turns. Though some of them did what birds do, they lay down and pretended to be lame.

Finally all three of them, Önde and Borne and Könik, had each driven a rabbit into Tvare's cow-shed. When they had killed them they stood still and looked at one another. They were soaked in blood and panting heavily, and Borne said: "They never imagined this would happen to them."

But Önde and Könik said nothing, they were having to tense their muscles till their whole bodies quivered, just to be able to stand still.

Tvare's two cows were in there. They were two of the cows they'd all continued to feed and milk and look after for those who had died, for no one. And the heifer as well, that Borne had appropriated. They had been out earlier in the day, but now they'd gone back to their shed of their own accord and were waiting for Eira to come and milk them. They stood chewing the cud of the poor grass from the forest.

Then Önde went out for a while. When he came back he had an axe in his hands, one of those broad-bladed ones that Yvar used to make. And with a mighty blow of the axe-head he felled one of the cows, the one called Lena: he struck her on the forehead and she dropped down as if her hooves and legs had sunk straight through thin ice.

And this too was a signal for Borne and Könik. Könik took the axe out of Önde's hands and slaughtered the other cow, the one called Harda.

Borne killed the heifer himself.

And Könik found a sledgehammer inside Tvare's house.

That afternoon they killed twenty milking cows, twelve calves, fifteen sheep, an unknown number of goats, two boars, five sows and eighteen piglets – and that was more animals than all of them together had ever killed before in the whole of their lives.

Könik was not running now, he was walking calmly and dispassionately from house to house and slaughtering. He was a skilful man and did his job well; he didn't stop to think – he was fully occupied with his handiwork. But if he had thought anything it would have been: These wretched beasts have sinned against what is right and proper by being superfluous; they are damaging and destroying Creation, or rather, overfilling it to bursting point with their futility; they're disrupting what's appropriate and fitting, and upsetting the balance in Kadis so that we're all reeling and on the point of collapse. Their lives offend against logic and reason: it's better for them to be allowed to die. And he would also have thought: Everything moves inexorably onwards, but in what direction and towards what end, that's entirely uncertain.

Finally he came up to Evan's sow, whose name was Pila, the one who had borne his own boar, Blasius. He stood and took aim with the sledgehammer. Pigs have to be hit right in the middle between the ears quite high up.

But Önde arrived just at that instant and yelled out: "Do you know what she's called?"

Könik lowered the hammer. He was covered in blood from his hair right down to his feet and he was breathing heavily because he'd begun to tire. "No," he said, "I've never thought about it."

"She's called Cecilia," Önde said.

Könik scrutinized the sow. She was the fattest of all the animals he had faced that day.

"Who gave her that name?" he asked.

"Either Evan or I," said Önde, "I can't quite remember."

"I shan't kill her," said Könik.

"And şhe's the mother of your Blasius," said Önde.

"I wasn't really thinking about what I was doing," said Könik.

"It's like a web, the whole thing," said Önde. "Or like a woven wicker basket. Or like making a salmon net."

"I don't suppose I would have killed her," said Könik.

And so the sow was allowed to live: it seemed only right and proper that she should be saved – perhaps it was because of her name – and in due course she grew almost unbelievably old. Only much later, when this story nears its end, did she die of old age.

Borne joined them in the cow-shed. And he saw that they had spared the sow.

"What about her?" he said.

"No," said Könik.

And he added: "That's enough. We've come to our senses again. We can't possibly bring about any more order and harmony and more confusion and discord now than we already have.

"Everything looks absolutely dreadful all around us," he went on.

And it was true: there was blood flowing everywhere and corpses lying all over the place.

So Borne fetched a rope and they began to drag the slaughtered animals to the open square in front of the chapel. They helped one another with the heaviest beasts; the sheep and lambs and goats and piglets they carried in their arms. They looked like the shepherds that the priest had had on a scroll in the chapel. They piled the bodies on top of one another and hooked bones and necks and heads round each other to give stability to the edifice. It turned into a mountain of bodies, it looked like a huge stock of stumps for tar-making or a mound of the most misshapen stones. And as they raised this mournful cairn it began to get dark. So Önde brought some tar-sticks and they got fire from Bera's house. Then they went on working in the light from the torches; none of them wanted to call it a day until they'd done what they intended to do. If a stranger had come and seen them he would almost certainly have thought that they were celebrating some kind of festival in the darkness. The flaming torches dipped and swayed and moved hither and thither through Kadis. And it was about the time of hay-making and digging up the first turnips, so it was the right time for a harvest festival.

Last of all they tried gathering up the rabbits.

But that was hard. The rabbit corpses were small and hidden in the grass. Neither Borne nor Önde nor Könik could remember any more where they'd thrown them. And it was such a terribly long time ago. If anyone had asked them when it was that they were hunting the rabbits they would have said: "Well, we remember doing it, but when it was is completely impossible to remember: it was after supper one day towards the end of summer."

They gave up when Könik happened to grab a live rabbit instead of a dead one, and they went down to the banks of the stream. They didn't undress. Könik was carrying the rabbit on one arm, and in the other hand he was holding the tar-stick

.torch. When they lowered themselves into the water the torches went out. They crouched down on their haunches the way they used to do when they were children, they sat completely still and let the water rinse them clean as best it could. Könik and Önde were shivering and shaking, but not Borne.

Könik took the rabbit home with him to Eira. He carried it over to the fire so that she could see it: it was a doe. It lay completely unafraid in Könik's hands; there was dark dried blood that the water hadn't been able to dissolve on his knuckles and round his nails and in the crease of his thumb.

"She's got a belly full of young'uns," he said. "And she seems happy and contented."

And he added: "I think she looks like you."

Eira started to laugh so much that she had to clasp her hands together for support under her stomach. She looked at the twitches on the rabbit's face and understood exactly what Könik meant, and Könik too burst out laughing. He couldn't control himself at all as he looked back and forth between Eira and the rabbit and heard her unrestrained laughter. They laughed so much, the two of them, that Könik was forced to put the rabbit down and lean against the wall. And of course he was very tired. Finally Eira had to lie down on the bed – her laughter was turning into cramp. She mustn't allow the rabbit and the merriment to cause her to give birth before her time.

These were the creatures that were still alive: Önde's cow and her calf; Bera's goats; Borne's own cow and the two cows he was looking after for Germund, who was dead; Ädla's cows and calves; Evan's sow that was now Önde's; Könik's cow; Jalte's bull, that Onde had taken over; an uncountable number of rabbits. That was all that remained after the men had delivered Kadis from the superfluity of animals.

And also Könik's and Eira's boar Blasius.

He was already bigger than his old father had been – he was taller than any pig had ever been before him in Kadis. He was really putting on weight, and it wasn't only because his flesh was growing so fast that he was covered in great folds of fat rippling back and forth over his back like waves whenever he moved – no, his whole bone structure was also getting bigger and bigger. He was as broad as a horse across the chest, and so high on his legs that his heavy male organ swung free even when he stood half-buried in his own filth up to his knees.

He didn't eat just the food Eira brought him three times a day. Önde and Ädla and even Bera often carried over tubs or buckets of stale food and sour milk or turnips or carrots that they'd boiled for him while the pot was still hanging over the fire. They would stand with him and scratch the back of his fat neck and talk to him and admire him; they used baby talk with him as if he were a child – and indeed he was the last to have been born in Kadis for a long time. And when he received their gifts and listened to their voices turning so strangely high-pitched and squeaky, the bristles rose all over his body as if he were trying to object to all this affection, as if he wanted to show them something of the toughness and the darkness lurking deep in his being.

But for those who visited him he was not just Blasius: he also represented something other than himself, he was something which was growing and becoming better and better, he bore witness to future times, he would thrive and perhaps also in due course bear fruit. Önde told him: "If the sow, your mother, is to be covered again, you're the only one who can do it."

Önde also taught him tricks: holding a little turnip on his snout and tossing it up and catching it again in his teeth, and sitting on his mighty haunches with his forelegs in the air and grunting in short bursts so that he sounded like a barking dog. In fact as a piglet he had looked in many ways just like a puppy.

Blasius gave off warmth like a stone that has been lying for a long time in the sun. There was always a white cloud of steam rising from his sty at dusk. That was probably why the rabbits liked Blasius. They gathered around him, especially at night-time, and they dug paths and burrows in the ground beneath him and in his dung and in the straw. When he lay down to sleep they pressed up against his back and crept in between the hanging folds of flesh on his neck and his front legs. The most daring of the youngest ones tried in vain to suckle from him. And he let them carry on. The world and Creation encompassed rabbits too, and the primeval power that had brought him into being had also created rabbits, they were probably some kind of undeveloped brothers and sisters, and he let his warmth flow over them. Once when Eira brought the food for him she saw two rabbits riding on his back as he ran to and fro in the sty.

But occasionally he would take a rabbit. Then he would simply give a quick flick of his head and swallow one of them, any of them. It happened so quickly that the victim had no time to be aware of it. His jaws would make a few champing movements and then it would all be over. And the other rabbits took no notice of what had occurred: it was an accident, or the small price they had to pay for Blasius' warmth. They might perhaps have averted their gaze respectfully for a moment. For them too the individual little life was completely without significance, the personal identity consisted at most of black tufts on the ears or a few oddly coloured strands of fur on the back, nothing more. For rabbits the family and the line were the only things that meant anything, the species had to be saved from the jaws of death. No attention need be paid to the loss of an individual life as long as the greater thing, the essential being of the rabbit, could be saved and propagated.

Önde and Borne and Könik in their unreasoning slaughter had cut and pruned Kadis to a size that fitted them again; they had freed themselves from the burden of that inhuman superfluity; seized by madness they had done the only sane thing. Now they had what they needed: milk from their own cows, fish from the river, barley and carrots and turnips, animals in the forest. And the rabbits.

The next morning steam was still rising from the mound of corpses, but it soon abated. For the first few days they were able to take all the meat they wanted, pieces of leg and back and tongues. And Eira boiled two whole pigs for Blasius. But then the bodies began to ferment: they hadn't been gutted and drained of blood, and their bellies were swelling in the warmth of the sun so that some of the animals appeared to be moving again, and there was a dreadful stench. And Könik decided that everything should be burned, despite Önde saying: "That won't be necessary, we'll get used to it; it's an unusual smell but not dangerous. By next summer decay and the foxes will have taken the lot."

They stuck dry firs into the mountain of meat and heaped twigs and branches and trunks over the top, they filled all the gaps they could reach with bark, and they fetched fire from Önde's house and set light to the whole disgusting pile.

But when the fire had consumed all that was combustible, the carcasses of the animals still lay there almost untouched. Just a few ears and tails were charred and the smell of burnt bristles and skin wafted over the whole of Kadis.

So they began again: trunks and branches and twigs and bark.

They kept the fire going for six days, and not until the seventh was most of it burned. There remained just a heap of backbones and skulls. But even that was a considerable mound.

The air was completely still during these few days, and the weather was warm and heavy. The smoke from the fire spread out over Kadis and just hung there. It was yellowy brown and had a sweet yet bitter taste; it obscured the sun so that it became impossible to distinguish the hours of daylight from one another; it clung to every object and to the bodies of both people and animals. When the women who'd stayed inside the houses scratched their cheeks or eyelids a yellow mass stuck to their fingertips, a sticky soot that resembled tar. Blasius, trying to roll free of the smoke, was covered in layer upon layer of straw and dung, so that he started to look like a bear. And the men had to grope their way between the houses, they could only see a few steps in front of them. The smoke was even settling out in the forest, so it was left to chance which trees were felled and dragged to the fire.

Onde and Borne cursed the smoke. But Könik bore it with patience: for him it was simply right and true. In the smoke the world showed itself as it really was. He was familiar with this darkness – yes, he was pleased that the others too would see Kadis as it had now actually become.

Könik didn't even bother to cough. But the others coughed – Borne had such bouts of hacking coughs that he had to go off behind a bush or creep in under a raised storehouse and vomit.

And Ädla coughed so much that she began to go into labour.

It was Könik who happened to be passing. He heard weeping and whimpering of a kind he hadn't heard since people stopped dying, and he groped his way in to her. She was lying on the bed, and when he felt over her with both hands he realized immediately how things were. She was coughing and moaning so wretchedly that the helplessness that usually felt like an aching abscess in his chest rose up into his throat and almost prevented him breathing.

And he thought: We must try to remember this – that Ädla gave birth to Avar's child when we burned the animals that had died.

Then he went to fetch Eira as fast as he could.

But when Eira came to Ädla and felt her, and saw her lying there both knotted up and gaping open, and heard her frightful labour cough, she was so terrified that her whole body began to shake, a stab of pain shot through her belly as if she herself were smitten with Ädla's labour pains, and she put her hands over her ears and ran home again bent double and snuffling.

So there was no one left for Könik but Önde.

"You're never at a loss," said Könik. "You can turn your hand to absolutely anything. You never make any distinction."

And Önde didn't even need any light from tar-sticks, he could do whatever was needed in the densest darkness, he always could, there was nothing for him that was ever irritatingly wrong or incomprehensible.

The baby's head was already out and he took hold of it with both hands and delivered Ädla, and he bit off the umbilical cord with his teeth. He tore up a piece of cloth – he didn't know what it was, but it was the mother's old skirt that Ädla's rabbits had lived in – and he wrapped the baby in it. Then he heard Ädla say, in a weak and miserable voice, still coughing all the time: "His name will be Avar."

Then Önde remembered that he had forgotten to see what sort of child Ädla had borne, Avar's child and grandchild, the heir she had managed to give birth to in there in that dreadful smoke. So he opened the cloth that he had wrapped around it and put his hand in and felt with his finger. Then he said:

"She can't be called Avar."

And Ädla didn't proffer another name. As if she thought that in these circumstances a girl might just as well be nameless.

He laid her down with Ädla and she took her up and put her to her breast, and when Önde heard the newborn baby start to smack its lips and suck he went out to the other men and carried on with the endless, nauseating burning.

The smoke lay over Kadis for six days like a tar-laden fog.

Eira looked after Ädla and the child. But Ädla didn't need much looking after. She hadn't been particularly harmed by the birth and was soon on her feet again. It was as if she had been specially designed to give birth to Avar's child, as if her body and the child's head had in some mysterious way been made to measure for each other.

When the mountain of animals had finally been roasted and melted down so that only backbones and skulls remained, Ädla was there with the child in a basket against her breast. Önde had made the basket. She stood and watched the men loading the charred bones on to Avar's hay-cart and pulling them down to the river bank, load after load. They heaved the whole lot out into the water. Some sank, and some floated gently and almost hesitantly off towards Umeå and the sea.

And Könik could still recognize every scrap of bone, his eyes had that special ability – that had been Yvar's cow and that had been Evan's bull-calf and that was once Tvare's boar. He didn't know himself how his eyes worked, a simple shape or line was enough for him to recreate with a feeling of shame and dismay the whole of the creature that had been destroyed. But he said nothing to Önde or Borne – how could they have understood – no, not even to Eira.

But suddenly Önde said: "Do you remember when we were little and used to drive them all to the forest and they had bells on their collars?"

Nobody else on earth was as innocent as Önde.

Könik took two steps towards him and thrust out his chest and yelled so loud that his voice gave way: "No, I don't!"

And he pressed his clenched fist against Önde's ribs, against his heart, and went on: "I can't remember that we ever did that, and especially not the collars and the bells."

As was his wont, Önde understood everything and nothing. So he just gave Könik a calm and steady smile, he said no more, and gradually Könik shrank back down again and became his usual self, and they were able to proceed with the last load.

Over the next few days Könik worked on the swinging seat he had promised Avar, a little chair that he fixed to the end of a pole that was bent round so that the whole structure looked like a human arm with the seat as the hand; and he hung it from a beam on Ädla's ceiling.

But the daughter of Ädla and Avar was given a name anyway: she was to be called Maria. It was Önde who gave her the name. Könik never used it – for him the child was a mistake and an aberration that could never be encompassed in a name.

And Könik finished the room that he was building on the side of his house, and Eira hung a curtain made of sheepskin over the opening between the room and the house. But the room was not the room that Könik had imagined. Everything was like that for him now.

And Blasius went on growing and thriving.

Bera was no longer alone with her goats. Borne had moved in with her. He came one evening and then stayed sitting there as dusk fell – yes, even when the darkness of night came.

"The question of teeth doesn't bother me," he said.

"What teeth?" Bera asked.

"The ones you haven't got," said Borne.

"How do you know anything about my teeth?" asked Bera.

"Everyone knows," said Borne. "The whole of Kadis knows. You hold your hand in front of your mouth so that it doesn't show."

"Everyone?" said Bera.

"Yes," said Borne. "Everyone."

"I've never thought about it," said Bera. "But now that you mention it . . . Though it could happen to anyone."

"As I said, it doesn't bother me," said Borne.

"I'm not really very old," Bera said. "I might still get some teeth."

Then they were silent. Yvar had made little bells for Bera's goats. They were tinkling.

Eventually Bera said: "I think it's dreadful, all that you've done."

"What have I done?" said Borne.

"You've done what nobody else wanted to do," said Bera.

"Someone has to do it," said Borne. "It could happen to anyone."

"How many people have you hanged and how many have you chopped the heads off with the axe?" Bera asked.

"I'm not really very old," said Borne. "It can't be very many."

"But it's dreadful," said Bera.

"I've never thought about it," said Borne.

And they were silent again for a good while.

"Though really it doesn't bother me," said Bera.

And so from that evening onwards they slept together.

And Önde moved in with Ädla. He brought his cow and calf with him, and Jalte's bull. And also something else that Ädla wasn't to see, a leather pouch that was full of something heavy and jingling, which he buried in the earth of the floor beneath Ädla's bed.

"Maria, she'll need some sort of father anyway," he said.

And Ädla remembered how it had all happened and thought that it wasn't too bad if Önde could be some sort of father.

But he had to sleep in a corner on his own.

"Once was enough and more than enough," said Ädla.

Önde couldn't fathom those words, he worried about them a lot. That she never wanted to experience anything so abhorrent again. That she remembered so well how Maria was conceived and that any repetition was superfluous. Or that no one could ever be as Avar had been.

And Önde complied. He never tried to lay his hands on her or force himself into her bed. But once he said to her: "There are people who know the most essential things without being told, and who get everything for nothing. Like my half-brother

127

Jasper. He knew that he had a woman in Nordingrå and that she was slightly knock-kneed and had close-set eyes and a little gap between her front teeth and he would only have to go and fetch her."

"You had Cecilia," Ädla said.

"What do you know about Cecilia?" asked Önde.

"You and she lived together, and the priest had joined you."

"Yes," said Önde. "I remember."

"That was for always," said Ädla.

"Nothing can be for always," said Önde.

"I don't know," said Ädla.

"Nothing is permanent," said Önde. "I can't think of anything more futile and vain than things that are permanent. Things that are for ever, I can do without. Stones in the earth, they'll last for ever, and so will Scree Hill. When I think about things that last for ever, I get such an ache in my whole body that I have to get up and run several times round Kadis."

He listed the names of relations and neighbours that the Sickness had taken. And went on:

"Everything should be as it happens naturally. I never resist. Trying to stop things is like pissing on a forest fire. Things go the way they're meant to go."

He would never have dared speak like that if Könik had been listening to him.

And he told her exactly what had happened with Cecilia. A fur trader had come.

That's how simple it was, that's how simple everything was. That was the wisdom he had acquired and the rule he lived by: there'll always come a fur trader or something like it.

"Did you take any payment for her?" asked Ädla.

Önde appeared to ponder for a moment.

"I can't remember," he said. "But if I did, it certainly wasn't much."

But Könik couldn't help going over to rebuke Bera and Borne. He came late one evening when they'd already gone to bed. When he thought about them he couldn't sleep, he said. They were living as man and wife without being so. No priest had joined them. No handshakes had been exchanged between their fathers. No celebration had been held, they had just paired off like animals in the forest. And was Bera really lawful? – not all the parts of her body were yet fully grown. And hadn't Borne sinned so dreadfully against Creation that by rights he should never touch a woman at all?

When they had listened to him for long enough, Borne got up and took hold of him. He put his arms around him as if he were a tree trunk from the forest and carried him home to Eira and laid him down in the bed beside her.

Yes, a lot of things happened, and a lot got done. Borne also carried the devil that Könik had hewed and carved to the chapel – Könik didn't want to do it, he wouldn't touch it any more.

Ädla and Bera salted down rabbits and hares that Önde and Borne trapped. And ten barrels of fish of all kinds.

Borne went to Umeå and exchanged Bera's goat cheeses for more salt and a long rope; his old one had gone when they were dealing with the animals.

And they gathered in hay and leaves when the time came; the creatures that were left would really be able to eat day and night if they wanted to.

The men brought back firewood from the forest.

Borne cleaned out the lock-up and repaired the lock. The lock-up was the smallest house in Kadis but had the thickest walls. That's where they used to put people who had offended in various ways when there was still an order to offend against. It was by the wall on the way to the burial ground. The bar to go across the door was broken, so he made a new one from a fir tree from up by the edge of the bog. It was as thick as his own thighs and so heavy that only he could handle it; even Önde couldn't.

But Könik did nothing now, or almost nothing: he was waiting for Eira to give birth. None of them knew when her time was really due, but she had probably already gone past it. She was so heavy that she could hardly walk. Könik was with her all the time. All she could do was feed Blasius, but even that tired her dreadfully. Könik carried the buckets for her and poured the food in the trough. What she did was to say: "Eat up now, Blasius." She performed some of the gestures of feeding and spoke the ritual phrases and gave a kind of blessing to the eating itself.

Only on one single occasion did Könik leave Eira on her own. He went to the forest with Borne to collect self-seeded saplings for sledge runners.

That was when Eira gave birth.

But Önde was there, who else? – he'd brought a pot of boiled fish for Blasius – and all went well. She gave birth so simply and easily that she hardly even needed to bear down.

So when Könik came back from the forest the baby was already swaddled and lying in Eira's arms.

Önde undid the cloth so that Könik could look.

It was a son. Könik lifted him up and gazed at him as if he were an object that something special could be carved out of. He was a strong child and cried and whimpered so loudly that it brought tears to Könik's eyes. On his back just below the waist he had a fiery-red birthmark and on his head he already had thick, dark brown hair. Könik laid him down again and wrapped the cloths round him himself and gave him back to Eira.

When Önde had gone – he went when he saw that he was no longer needed – Eira and Könik began talking about a name for their son. They found large numbers of names in their memories that no one had any use for any more. But when one of them said a name, any name at all, Könik could see the man who had had that name, or could hear his voice. He sat on the stool by Eira's bed and the ghosts came and went: they sat at the foot of

130

the bed or leaned against the door-post or warmed their hands momentarily over the embers.

The man who was really the only one who knew how to make nets. The man who could recite three prayers by heart. And the man who always sat mending the nets. The man who had known how everyone was related to everyone else. And the man who'd been able to carve signs for all these names. And the only man who could tell the difference from the perspective of eternal judgement between murder and theft and fornication. The man who knew the times when animals were on heat or pregnant. The two men who had watched that no one was careless with fire. And the man who could turn a calf the right way round in the cow's womb. The man who had counted time on wooden pegs.

And numerous others who had left their names vacant.

Finally Könik had to creep in with Eira, to lie against her back, and seek protection from all those names.

And she could feel him trembling and realized immediately what was wrong. She usually knew word for word what Könik was thinking.

This was what Könik was thinking: Should he go out into life dressed in a name belonging to someone else? Is there no end to the disorder and confusion, must he be a stealer of names, couldn't they call him quite simply The Son?

She also knew that Könik would never be able to bear to possess something as nonsensical as a son without a name. So she said:

"Kare."

She took it out of empty nothingness. No one had been called that in Kadis before. And Könik immediately stopped shaking. "Yes, of course," he said, "Kare," as if nothing had been more natural than that name. "We found an answer to the problem this time, anyway."

*

Something remarkable was happening to Blasius. Eira had always tried to keep him clean, every day she'd poured a bucket or two of water over him, but now he'd got really filthy again. He never remembered that he ought to scrub himself against the palings of his sty. Now that Eira was fully occupied with Kare, Könik had often thought that he ought to make Blasius clean and tidy again. But he didn't get round to it. There were such a frightful lot of things that were wrong. So why should he bother particularly with Blasius?

He had a thick layer of all kinds of filth over his whole body, dung and straw and bits of food, and the food was mostly fish. This thick crust of muck and waste had begun to ferment, or rather to glow. It was the result of his extraordinary body-heat. Blasius became luminous. Late in the evenings he would begin to give off a glimmering blue-green iridescence. And they would all come and stand looking at him, they were convinced they were seeing a miracle. But Könik thought that this was just what might have been expected. When the world breaks up and disintegrates, miracles are only right and proper. If someone thinks up a fiction or a tall story in which he entraps both animals and men, one or another of them is bound to be afflicted like this. It would have been more inexplicable if Blasius had not become luminous, a pig of light.

But Eira, who'd noticed before how rubbish and old fish could glow, just said that they should scrub him clean, and when Önde did so, Blasius became himself again. But then Könik was almost frantic, he wanted to see the truth, he didn't want it washed away with water and a scraper.


Yes, while the others thought they were managing, that they were even managing better day by day, everything was getting worse and worse for Könik. Even his son was no consolation to him: he was a source of joy beyond all reason, but his rightful place was not in Kadis.

And he wanted to explain things to Eira.

Now the wolves had taken five of Bera's goats. Before, they would all have gone out with the wolf-net. Before, the seasons had come in the right order and at the right time – indeed, the people of Kadis had even watched over the seasons and known how to call them up if necessary. Now there was nobody who bothered. The water in the gully was yellow now. Before, Enar had come and made it clear again. Before, the paths between the houses had been kept tidy and as they should be. Now they were overgrown and paths appeared just anywhere. Now the posts were rotting in the walls. Before, they would have changed them for new ones immediately. Before, everyone had decided everything together. Now they sowed and harvested and slaughtered at any time and any-where. Now there were two newborn babies. Before, the priest would have come to scoop water on to them, and Oda to smear their navels and eyelids with horse-fat.

He could go on like that for hours, night after night.

"But even so," said Eira. That encompassed all she knew: "But even so." She had known that all her life.

Könik always had to mention Önde too. His name-sign was now carved everywhere. Every day on yet another house or a sledge or a cart or a storehouse or an axe-shaft or on another cattle-shed or a drying-shed – yes, everywhere where the two notches with the cross-hatch could be carved. And again Eira would say: "But even so." But she could hear for herself that there were circumstances where those two words were not suf-ficient.

Könik, then, had a deep furrow in his brow. It went straight down from his hair-line to the bridge of his nose. He had been born with it. It even went on down over his nose and ended on the point of his chin. It was like a sign that someone had carved without asking him, and it split his face into two halves. The two sides of his face seemed not to belong together at all: one was as if cut from a birch trunk, hard and unmoving, the other was like damp leather, soft and floppy. One eye was dry and wide open, the other was half-closed and watery so that he was constantly having to wipe it with his wrist. Eira used to put her forefinger on the furrow and stroke his brow.

Sometimes she would use all her fingers and knead and rub his brow to smooth out the line between his right face and his left face, between the bitter side and the despairing side. And it really did help on occasion: the skin and flesh would soften and yield to her fingertips, she could massage the real Könik out to his forehead and cheeks and skin the way you can massage the blood to a frozen part of the body.

And then something would happen that Könik didn't understand.

He would close his eyes and after a while a bright light would appear on the inside of his eyelids, at first rather sharp and stinging, but then it would soften and become more like the afternoon sun. It must have been finely streaked with blood, but he was pleased and warmed by it, and finally he always fell asleep. She would take his head on her lap, and the light would turn imperceptibly into sleep.


And when he awoke, everything would be normal again.

One morning – it was uncertain what season it was, but there was new snow – he was finally going to sort everything out with Önde. Some things must be stopped, anyway. He'd promised Avar that he'd keep an eye on Önde.

Önde was not just Önde. He was disorder and confusion. He was the paths that were overgrown and the water that had turned yellow and the time that had disintegrated, he was the Sickness that was still active in Kadis. He was the devil himself.

Ädla was not at home. She had gone to Bera's and taken the baby that for Könik had no name. Önde was sitting on Avar's old stool that Könik's father had hewn out of the great trunk of a fir tree.

"The money you took from Olavus the trader," Könik said, "where is it now?"

"Those bits and pieces," said Önde. "I can't even remember."

"It's not yours," said Könik.

"I was only looking after it," said Önde. "Someone had to."

"We must restore order for that man Olavus," said Könik. "We must throw the money in the river."

"If I hadn't been good to him and taken him in," said Önde, "he would never have died here in Kadis."

"We must restore order in everything," said Könik.

"The whole of Kadis," he went on, "is crumbling to pieces, like a lump of clay when you hit it."

"Order," said Önde. "That's not something you can make. Not like a stool or a table. Order makes itself."

"When I had to carve that devil for the chapel," said Könik, "he turned out like you, whatever I did."

"Yes," said Önde, "that's what I mean."

"You're putting your mark on everything," said Könik. "On houses and sledges and store-sheds."

"It happens so easily," said Önde. "I'm practising. My hand and the knife just do it, whatever I mean to do."

He pulled his knife out of the sheath he had hanging against his thigh and ran his thumb along the blade.

"And you hide things and bury things," said Könik.

"Then at least they're still there," said Önde.

"You're taking over the whole of Kadis and misappropriating it," said Könik. "If there were any justice, we would be compelled to hang you."

"Yes," said Önde and looked down at his knife. "That may be true."

"I won't want to live any longer," said Könik, "if we can't hang you one fine day."

Önde made no reply to that. And Könik yelled: "Where have you buried the silver, you devil?"

135

"I'm sure you know," said Önde. "You know me so well that you don't need to ask. And it's not just silver."

So Könik heaved aside Ädla's bed and got down on his knees and began to dig, he dug with both hands and threw the earth around him wildly. Önde shielded himself to protect his eyes. And Könik soon found what he was looking for: it was a shallow pit, like the sort you make for laying down fish. Yes, he found not only what he was seeking, but much more besides. There were leather pouches and things wrapped in bits of cloth, and there was a dried stomach filled with something and two little wooden boxes which Könik recognized – he had made them for Avar. No indeed, it wasn't just silver. Everything that Avar had had was there in the pit, and also everything else that Önde had been able to find that might have belonged to just about anybody, everything that those poor dead people had managed to collect and that Könik never knew existed. This was the legacy of the whole of Kadis.

But Könik was not even man enough to touch it, his hands knotted up with cramp when he tried.

Then he got up and took out the knife he'd had under his shirt. And he was so confused that he cried out, "I'm going to strangle you!" despite the fact that it was quite obvious he was going to use the knife.

Önde sat quite still and looked at him as if it was nothing to do with him what Könik did in his anger. But then he quickly turned the knife in his hand and threw it into the wall behind him – the knife was either a hindrance or a temptation to him – and with three agile leaps he was past Könik and out through the doorway before either of them realized what was happening. He rushed down towards the river and then followed the bank upstream, and Könik was ten paces behind him. They were both running for their lives. Their heads were empty of thoughts, they were simply hurtling along, chance and disorder in front, order and justice behind, and when they came to the first lake, they turned into the forest, up the mountainside.

They had raced one another on numerous occasions, they were a perfect match: the ten paces remained ten even if Önde sometimes leapt sideways like a rabbit and Könik tried to take a short cut round a rock or tree or past a pool. Nor did it make any difference that one of them was empty-handed and the other had a long-bladed knife in his hand. It wasn't really Könik's knife but one of Yvar's, and that too was hateful for Könik. Yvar used to have it for splitting firewood, and he'd got it from Önde.

So they ran a good way along the bank and then through the undergrowth and up the hill on to the common. Neither of them worried about where they were getting their strength and stamina from or whether their breath would last, there wasn't time to worry, neither of them had any choice but to keep on with that terrible running.

But wherever the strength came from, it finally began to ebb, and they grew short of breath. By then they were right out in the wilds.

It was Önde who finally stopped. They had come out on to a hillside where the storms had flattened all the forest. He suddenly pulled up and turned round and Könik couldn't stop himself, he crashed into Önde and knocked him over so that they were both thrown headlong on to the bare earth beneath an uprooted tree. They held on to each other so firmly in the fall that they could hardly move their arms and legs when the fight itself began. Önde hit his shoulder on a rock, and a broken root ripped a great wound in Könik's cheek.

Könik still had the knife, but as closely intertwined as they were it mattered little who had it. The knife became a third party in the battle, sometimes cutting Önde, sometimes Könik.

As with the race, so with the fight. Since childhood they had fought innumerable times, they were equally matched; the result depended on who happened to get the better grip and who was momentarily more cunning with his hands and feet. Önde was perhaps stronger and nimbler, but Könik had greater stubbornness and more fear. Önde would sometimes lie down flat on his

137

back just to encourage Könik. They hadn't been able to draw breath after the race and now they were squeezing each other's chests empty, they didn't even have enough breath left to moan or groan, and all they managed to achieve with their fingers and heads and feet was to fasten so firmly on to one another that in the end all attempts at new holds were futile. The knife remained in motion longest, it aimed at their arms and thighs but spared their throats. Finally their fingers and legs and necks grew tired and weak and the knife fell to the ground and Önde and Könik fell asleep in each other's arms.

When Önde woke, the sun had already passed midday. He freed himself from Könik – they hadn't loosened their grip in sleep and it took him a good while to disentangle his arms and legs from Könik's. He was covered in wounds, but the blood had stopped flowing. And he could move all his limbs. When he looked Könik over he saw that the knife had cut off his right ear.

But Könik wasn't bleeding either – it was the cold. He tried to wake him: Könik wouldn't have the strength today to try to kill him again. But Könik couldn't be woken. He was sleeping as if after a hard day's work – he was even snoring.

So Önde picked him up and put him over his shoulders and started for home.

His wounds were sore, his legs were still stiff from the run and the fight, and the newly-fallen snow was treacherous under his feet. He walked slowly to save his strength but he walked as fast as he could to get home to Kadis before evening.

When he came down to the river dusk was beginning to fall. And now Könik woke. In his sleep he had seen a man carrying a wounded kid. And he realized immediately that it was he himself who was the kid. But he couldn't bring himself to tell Önde that he had woken.

Önde's steps were desperately tired and heavy, and from time to time he staggered. These steps of Önde's were the heaviest in Könik's life.

Önde opened the door to Könik's house with his foot. Eira had a fire going inside. He laid Könik carefully on the bed.

"We were out in the forest," he said to Eira, "and we came upon a stranger who had a knife, and he had a good try at killing us."

And he looked at Könik and discovered that he'd been crying, that the tears had washed away all the blood from his face, and he realized that Könik had been awake for some time. Then he gave a great, if rather exhausted, laugh – he was laughing at himself for having carried Könik and at Könik who because of his shame couldn't stop himself from being carried. But Eira understood straight away that it was no stranger they had met, but one another.

In the warmth indoors Könik's wounds began to bleed again. Blood was already flowing from Önde when they arrived. Eira made Önde lie down on the bed beside Könik, in her own place, and she brought some cold water and washed them and tore up two of Könik's old tunics to bind round the wounds. He never wore tunics any more since trousers had come to Kadis. She put a rabbit fur on the wound where his ear had been, so that it would be soft for him.


When Ädla came home with Maria and found the appalling disorder Könik had caused she stood for a while in thought. Then with her hands she raked back the earth over the pouches and skins and the dried stomach and put her bed to rights again. That must be what she was supposed to do.

When Önde had been looked after, he got up and went home to Ädla. Despite the fact that he didn't really get any pleasure from her. And to support Önde's story, Könik said to Eira: "That stranger we met when we were out in the forest had shaved off all his beard and he was a head taller than any man I've ever seen, and he had a woven band of silver threads over his forehead and hair."

So now Eira had three poor wretches to care for, three masters, she thought to herself. She would have to keep them clean and chatter to them and feed them and imbue them with her own fortitude. Without knowing why, she would get tears in her eyes in the presence of any one of them, Könik and Kare and Blasius.

önik stayed in bed while his wounds healed. When there was enough light he lay looking at Kare. Under his head Eira had placed a goatskin that she had stuffed with straw and soft hay, and Kare lay in the cradle that Könik had made for him before he was born, so if Könik turned his head and lay on the ear he still had he could see his son. And then he couldn't hear Kare screaming if Eira stayed too long with the cow or Blasius at any time.

Önde would come and sit with him for a while. His wounds had soon healed and he of course hadn't lost any part of his body, so Ädla didn't think there was any reason to carry on nursing him; but they never said anything to each other, Önde and Könik. It was as if everything had been said at the time they went running to the forest.

And Bera came. She no longer held her hand in front of her mouth when she spoke and she had combed out her hair and plaited it. She was going to have a child by Borne. Könik had never heard her laugh before, but she laughed often now, and it wasn't the bleating Könik had expected – no, she had a clear and musical laugh, and she was constantly occupied with the child she was going to have. She was sewing clothes for it and she was stuffing herself full with all the food she could get her hands on so that it wouldn't go hungry, and she talked about it all the time. First her child was going to be like one of the people who had lived in Kadis, then it would be like another. First it would resemble someone in one particular way, then someone else in another. Yes, she seemed to be grateful to the Great Sickness for having taken all the previous people so that their characteristics were available for her unborn child. She had lived alone with her goats in the old Kadis: the new Kadis had given her Borne, and a fertility that manifested itself not only in her womb but also in her cabbage patch and in the rabbits that she'd taken on, and in the goats that were giving twice as much milk as before, and in her speech, where the words came so fast upon one another that she herself couldn't hear or understand them all.

And Borne came to see Könik. He wanted to see his ear.

"What ear?" said Könik.

"The one you lost."

"It was left behind in the forest," said Könik.

"Taking an ear," said Borne, "that's not as easy as you'd think."

"Nothing's as easy as thought would have it," said Könik. "Thought is a braggart and compulsive liar."

"You'd have to slice diagonally from above," said Borne. "And one single cut. You wouldn't be able to hack and saw."

"All the people who really had particular skills are gone," said Könik. "The ones who knew things that no one else knew."

"You'd have to cut towards the bone," said Borne. "And mind the cheek. And you'd have to give the knife a sharp twist, or there'd be some of the gristle left."

And Könik had to unwind the cloth and the piece of rabbit fur so that Borne could see.

"Yes," said Borne, "it's really well done. He's a remarkable man, Önde, he can manage just about anything."

So Önde had told Borne everything.

"It wasn't Önde," said Könik. "The knife did it itself."

"Yes," said Borne. "That's exactly the art of it."

"But I've still got my hearing," said Könik. "I'd gladly be without both my hearing and my sight."

"There was never any question of your eyes," said Borne. "I've heard of it happening. But never here in Kadis."

142

And Könik put back the piece of rabbit fur and Borne helped him with the bandages.

"And it didn't even bleed very much," said Borne. "I must talk to Önde again."

It was while Könik was lying there in bed that he really began to love Kare.

He took after Eira. Those cheeks and that chin with a little dimple and those eyes and that upper lip that was slightly protruding and that snub nose. And his skin was pink and glowing like a cloudberry or like a freshly-skinned rabbit. He ought to have been luminous if anyone was. He often gurgled with happiness – yes, a kind of bliss flowed from him straight out into the empty nothingness around him. And he was completely helpless, he lay there waving his arms and legs in the air like a sign of impotence. Not to mention how innocent he was, and free from sin; he hadn't moved a single thing from its rightful place, he hadn't said a word that could have a wrong meaning, he had never thought a thought that could lead himself or anyone else astray.

But on his forehead and down on the bridge of his nose he had that deep furrow, he'd been born with that, he'd inherited it. And soon he would begin to think and speak and move things from their rightful place. Then the world would begin to fall apart and disintegrate around him. Because he would live here in Kadis. Even if he learned to handle tools, much more would be smashed and destroyed than he would manage to plane and fit together and construct. The movements of decline are swifter than those of creation, he would have to live in a period of disintegration – yes, he would probably contribute to it himself. That's how Kadis was now.

It would have been better if no one had begotten him, if no one had woken Eira from her paralysis and in a feverish confusion and with a momentarily unlined face caused him to be conceived. It would have been better for him if he'd suffocated inside Eira before he'd been born, it would be better if he died.

Yes, Könik lay there looking at Kare and worshipped him so much that his eyes began to swell up and turn red and suppurate. Eira fetched some sour beer from Ädla and bathed them with it.

The beer was from Avar's time. Ädla sometimes took a sip in the evenings to help her sleep. She couldn't get used to having Önde in the house. And the little girl Maria often cried out during the night.

But the beer didn't help against either Önde or the sleeplessness.

The first time Könik got up out of bed was one morning. It was cold and he had to do something about the fire. Eira was outside with Blasius. He was stiff and numb, and he could only get up by instructing one part of his body at a time. He didn't finally straighten up and stand properly on his two legs until he was over by Kare's cradle. His first steps were tottering ones. And somehow it came about that instead of going across to the fire he bent down and put his hands on Kare's chest. Kare was asleep. Then he stroked his poor little ribs and laid the palms of his hands on his shoulders, or what were meant to be his shoulders. And he raised his thumbs and brought his hands together so that Kare's neck ended up between his thumbs and forefingers. It was uncertain what his hands were actually up to.

But Kare woke up and began to scream in a frantic, infantile way, as if in fear for his life.

Just at that moment Önde came by. He had a cheese for Blasius, it was a cheese he had wanted to make for Ädla, but it had got maggots in. Önde cast the cheese down in the snow – the scream was too terrible to have come from such a little child – and pushed open the door and threw himself into the house: it was as if he'd been ready for that scream or something like it. And he jumped on to Könik's back and grabbed hold of his arms, he got his hands in under Könik's elbows and brought them together so that Könik was forced to let go his ambiguous hold on Kare's neck and stay pinioned in Önde's grip.

So they stood once again intertwined when Eira came back from seeing to Blasius. She stopped absolutely still in the doorway. She didn't say anything, but Önde could see her eyes searching for the knife.

"No," he said, "we haven't got the knife."

And he went on: "You needn't be frightened, I've got him."

She came in to them then.

"Könik," she said. "Könik."

But he didn't answer.

"You must fetch Borne," Önde said. "Go to Bera's quickly and fetch Borne."

Eira went up to the cradle and inspected Kare. Then she said: "He hasn't done anything. And I'll look after him."

"But he's dangerous," said Önde. "He's a danger to the whole of Kadis."

"I won't go," said Eira.

"I'll never set him free," said Önde. "So you might as well go."

"Apart from Könik," said Eira, "there's not a single just and faultless person."

Könik was groaning with the effort of trying to free himself from Önde's grip, and Önde was groaning with the effort of holding him.

"It's inescapable," Önde gasped. "And inevitable."

"You're always saying," said Eira, "that nothing is inevitable."

"You shouldn't pay any attention to one solitary expression," Önde almost screamed. "Inevitable is just a word."

"There's a cheese out there in the snow," said Eira.

"It's for Blasius," Önde groaned.

"No," said Eira again. "I'm not going."

But then Könik decided the whole matter.

"Go now," he said in a panting voice to Eira, "it's right, it's the only right thing to do, fetch Borne."

145

So Eira went to Bera's and fetched Borne.

And Önde and Borne dragged Könik off to the house called the lock-up. Borne held his legs and Önde his arms. It was a heavy and difficult task because Könik was struggling the whole time and trying to get himself free. They threw him inside on to the earth floor, where there was a pile of sheepskin covers. Önde had put them there just as if he'd foreseen that someone would soon be needing to keep warm in there. Borne put the terrible bar against the door and pressed it down into its slots.

And what was Eira to do?

She picked up Kare from his cradle and gave him her breast. Then she sat for a long time just holding him. Könik had once said that he would try to carve a picture of her sitting just like that. If she'd known a prayer, she would have said it.

She whispered to Kare that he shouldn't worry, Könik would soon be back with them again. She pressed him to her as if she had to hold on tight to him. She bent forward and huddled over him as if she wanted to enclose him in her womb again.

But in the end she put Kare down and went out and picked up the cheese that Önde had thrown down and took it to Blasius. It was so big and heavy that she had to use both hands. But for Blasius the cheese was just a tiny plaything. He threw it up on the top of his head and bounced it up and down on the front of his face below his eyes and let it roll down on to his snout where he held it balanced with tiny flicks of his head. Finally he sat on his haunches and held the cheese in his mouth. He was always like that, he never bothered to make any distinction between seriousness and play. So Eira had to clap her hands and call to him and say how clever he was – otherwise he probably wouldn't have bothered to eat it.

*Where there is justice, the water runs clear in the gully.*

önik tore the bandages from his arms and legs and head himself. His wounds had healed. There was no fireplace in there, there were only the sheepskins – he had five on top and five underneath him. Despite the darkness everything was very clear and easy to see. There was a hole in the wall that was big enough for a fist or a wooden bowl or a loaf. That's where Eira brought his food.

He didn't know how long he would be there, no one knew, no one even knew for certain what he'd done, there was no one to judge him. He'd been put in the lock-up for safety's sake, as a sensible temporary measure, as a precaution, almost at random or by accident. Borne came by every day and inspected the walls and the door: now he had a man to guard. When Könik awoke for the first time after having slept for a while, he no longer knew how long he'd been there.

No one knew the conditions that had to be fulfilled for him to be let out. For the moment they had him there, and not a word was said about the day and time when he could come out again. Önde and Borne had had to lock him up, that's all. Except for the times when he was eating, he lay in the pile of sheepskins.

On one occasion Önde said to Borne: "If we hadn't locked him up, we would never have needed to worry ourselves about setting him free."

What the others did while Könik was in the lock-up isn't significant; they themselves didn't think it was significant. They did everything that was necessary. Eira too, she milked the cows and made food and went backwards and forwards between her three poor wretches, Kare, Blasius and Könik, with jugs and bowls and dishes. Who would believe that she'd recently – or was it quite a long time ago – been lying paralyzed?

But during this whole time she didn't go to visit Ädla or Bera and they didn't come to her. After all, her Könik had tried first to kill Önde and then Kare.

Könik didn't say anything to Eira. Except once: he asked her for a piece of wood and the little knife he used for carving.

But she told him everything that was happening in the outside world: Kare's teeth and his first words; she'd heard that Bera had had a son; a rabbit had taken Könik's place in the bed; she'd put a cow-bell on Blasius.

Yes, Blasius could be heard ringing his bell right over here.

And that the snow was melting and disappearing.

No one knew what Könik was thinking. But one day when the year had advanced to the point when he no longer needed the sheepskin blankets, and when the cherry trees were about to blossom – perhaps he recognized the smell – he'd obviously finished thinking, because he told Eira to fetch the others, all the people of Kadis. And when they'd arrived he spoke to them through the hole in the wall:

"I'm glad that you've come here and are willing to listen to me. I haven't got very much to say, but the little I have to put to you comes from my heart. Nothing has really happened here in Kadis. Nothing is broken and nothing is missing. A few people died a while ago, we're not sure when, and we've buried them, and that's all. There are enough of us, we have enough animals and most of them are fat enough and we have enough food for our hunger. Everything is right and proper – yes, show me a single thing that isn't just right. Life is going on as usual. Law and order reigns. Anyone who wants can own what he wants and no one is guilty of anything. Kadis has become part of a story that someone is telling, we don't know who, and it's the most well-ordered and neat and harmless little story you can imagine. And it's completely just and right that I'm in here. It's my wish that you never let me out of here. That's all."

That's what Könik said through the opening, not word for word, but in broad outline.

And of course they couldn't keep a man imprisoned who talked like that.

So Borne lifted aside the bar and unlocked the door to let Könik out.

He walked with short little steps and hardly moved his head and his face was completely immobile and he was covered in sheep's wool and he had the little piece of wood in his hand that he had been carving.

And they were all pleased about the piece of wood, the image that he'd carved in his spare time in the shaft of light from the aperture. They could look at that instead of at Könik. Thanks to the piece of wood they could avoid a certain embarrassment that would otherwise have been a likely and normal response.

Even Eira admired that piece of wood that was somewhat smaller than the palm of her hand. And she was the only one who definitely recognized what it represented.

It represented Kare. But not Kare the baby – no, Kare as he would eventually turn out, as he would necessarily and naturally look in a few years' time. Of course he was still just a child, but his hair was cut round his ears and his eyes were slightly pinched together and the furrow across his brow had deepened and gave his face an almost painful seriousness. And Borne said:

"Who is that meant to be?"

"It's some kind of angel," said Ädla.

"I think I've seen him before," said Önde.

He couldn't know that he was seeing a person he hadn't yet seen, that perhaps none of them would ever see – everything was so uncertain.

"Jasper will look almost like that," said Bera. Jasper was the child she had had by Borne.

But Könik said nothing. He went home with Eira.

He really did walk with dreadfully short steps, he the man who had previously taken such long and sure strides. And he held his arms still at his side, he didn't even move his hands. And when they were alone so that he could finally say something, he hardly opened his lips and he more whispered than spoke.

"Is Kare all right?" he asked.

"Yes, he's asleep."

"Is everything as it should be with Blasius?"

"Yes, he'll be fed as soon as we get home."

And they could hear the cow-bell that Blasius had round his neck and that he used for calling Eira.

Könik's expression didn't change. She looked at him but he didn't smile, nor did he have any creases of despair in his face, apart from the furrow, of course. Both halves of his face were equally still and unlined. He also seemed to have become slightly stooped, perhaps from sitting bent over and carving Kare.

She had a soup of crushed barley and a rabbit over the fire. They ate.

He ate carefully like a child who's afraid of burning himself on the food or who doesn't want to spill it or who's eating only out of duty. He didn't touch the table with his elbows or fingers, he sat on the very edge of the stool as if he were going to get up again straight away; he didn't touch Eira, he didn't bend over Kare to kiss him and smell him.

He had not become paralyzed – no, he hadn't managed to go that far, but he had withdrawn and turned in on himself and slackened his pace in every way so that you could imagine the blood was congealing in his body. So he would never move an object from its rightful place, nothing would concern him and he wouldn't concern anybody or anything; nothing would impinge upon him and he would never think a thought that might change anything.

She'd heard somewhere that birds acted like that when hunters were after them.

But he threaded a leather thong through the figure he'd carved of Kare and hung it round his neck.

When they went to bed at night Könik lay by the wall where

he'd lain while Eira was like a bird. She'd made a bed for Kare in the box that Könik had slept in when he was a baby. She put it on Könik's side of the fire so that he would be able to reach it if he woke up in the middle of the night and forgot that he wasn't to touch anything. While Könik was in the lock-up Kare had slept in her bed. In the afternoon of the same day Önde went up into the forest. He wanted to see if the roach were playing, he was going to look for birds' eggs, he was going to cut birch bark, he was going to look for sundew plants that make sour milk fresh and take away warts. Yes, he was going to the forest for a thousand reasons that he told Ädla, and he'd be gone a few days. In fact he didn't need to say anything to Ädla: she didn't worry about his comings and goings, she was content to have Maria. The girl was crawling around now in the straw on the floor. She had white hair and large, surprised eyes, she could sit up straight and steady in the hanging seat that Könik had made, and she practised her first word over and over again, a sound that could have been either father or Avar, which anyway were one and the same.


When Eira woke up the next morning, Kare had gone. She stood for a while looking down into his empty box as if she thought her eyes were playing her tricks, then she thought: Könik must have come back to his senses in the night and felt he had to pick Kare up and take him on his arm and press him to his breast.

But in Könik's bed there was only Könik.

Then she began to scream and hit Könik to wake him, but he was sleeping incredibly heavily, and only when she pulled his hair and hammered on his chest with her fists did he open his eyes.

"Kare has gone," she cried.

"What do you mean?" Könik whispered.

"Kare has disappeared in the night."

Then Könik tried to creep under the blanket and turn to the wall, but she stopped him. She gripped hold of his shoulder and shook him to wake him up more. But he was probably as awake as he dared to be.

"He can't be far away," he said.

"He's gone," said Eira.

"He's gone out for a pee," said Könik.

"He can't walk yet," said Eira.

"Then I don't know," said Könik.

But now Eira took hold of him, small as she was, and lifted him up so that he was sitting in the bed, and she pulled him so hard that he almost fell out on to the floor.

"But don't you understand?" she screamed. "Don't you understand?"

"It may be," he said, "that I do understand. But what help is that?"

But she finally got him up out of bed and he got dressed. Yes, of course he would make an attempt to look for Kare, as well as you could look now in this impenetrable village of Kadis. She wasn't to think that he wasn't grieved by the loss of Kare.

"Grieved?" said Eira.

No, no, that wasn't what he meant, not that it was time to grieve for him; he just wanted her to know that he was as worried as she was.

"I shall get him back," said Eira defiantly.

"Yes," said Könik. "Of course you'll get him back."

And in fact he went right down to the river bank. He thought he could see fresh tracks from soles with two seams across. Someone had been half-running, with short steps, but he didn't look very carefully, he didn't dare look too carefully, and down at the water's edge the tracks disappeared.

Eira ran to the others, to Bera and Ädla, but no one had seen Kare, they had only just got up and hadn't yet seen a living soul and Önde had gone to the forest. If anyone had known anything

154

or been able to fathom out something, then it would have been Önde.

When Eira got back home Könik was with Blasius.

"He's like a miracle of God," he said.

"No one has seen him and no one knows anything," said Eira. "What shall we do?"

And she was crying, crying uncontrollably.

"He'll be wanting his food," said Könik.

When he mentioned food Eira shrieked in anguish. She still had milk in her breasts. And it took a while before she came to herself enough to be able to say: "Can it have been an animal?"

"No," said Könik. "There would have been blood everywhere."

He bent forward and scratched Blasius under his collar.

"How can you stand there?" said Eira in such distress that no one but Könik would have been able to make out her words. "How can you just stand there?"

"We can cook something for him later," Könik said. "But you could just give him a drop of sour milk."

And it was strange: Eira dried her face with the back of her hand and actually went and fetched some sour milk for Blasius.

Then the others came over to them. They stood on the grass between the carpenter's shop and the house, and hesitantly voiced their fears and suspicions about Kare. Ädla had her Maria in her arms and Bera had Jasper in a basket.

In reality they were all in silent agreement about what must have happened: someone had stolen Kare, someone who needed him himself or someone who was trading. Könik had told them that that sort of thing was going on in the world, children were being stolen and bought and sold like piglets or bundles of furs. And they looked at Könik – he was guilty of providing this knowledge, and therefore also for the anxiety and rage they were feeling. Yes, Könik was guilty.

Könik's face was still and unmoved. The furrow in his brow

was no deeper than usual. This was after all how the situation was now in Kadis.

"You could go to Umeå," said Bera to Borne. "It's sure to be someone from Umeå."

So that was what was done: Borne took three barley cakes and half a goat's cheese in a leather bag and went off to Umeå.

The others had jobs that had to be done. Eira got on with hers too – she milked the cow and cooked food for Könik and Blasius and she even lay for a good while in the cabbage patch and weeded, but she did it all as if in her sleep. She got up from time to time and stood absolutely still, with just a twitch and a tremor in her face and limbs.

It was evening before Borne came back. And Bera and Ädla came over.

Yes, it was quite right, a man had come down into town, and he'd had a little boy he'd been trying to sell. But the world was teeming with children again now: such times were long past. He'd never be able to find a buyer in Umeå, especially since no one could know anything certain about the child; it might well have some serious affliction that would make it useless later on. No, this man was someone who was living in the past and was stupid and ill-informed – he could be grateful that they hadn't arrested him in Umeå and hanged him.

And what then had the man done with the child?

Well, he'd been ferried across the river and gone off to the south, he must have been very disappointed. When Borne had heard that, he'd turned round and come back home again. It was pointless going any further through the country, there was no end to the world down to the south.

But what had the man looked like?

No, Borne hadn't bothered to ask that. He wasn't going to look any further for him, so why should he strain his memory to remember something that was of no use?

And the child?

Well, it was an ordinary sort of child, rather like Kare. No one in Umeå had mentioned there being anything special about him, nor had it been particularly important, because nobody was asking for children any more.

"But what if it had been your and Bera's Jasper?" said Eira in a plaintive and desperate tone.

"Who would steal him?" said Borne. "Nobody would dare because everyone knows that I'd go to the end of the world."

And Könik said very softly and carefully: "Anything at all can happen to anybody. Anything at all."

So Ädla and Bera and Borne went back home. They said nothing, they didn't know any words of consolation that they could use; they tried to leave quietly and gently so that Eira and Könik wouldn't notice them going.

Eira cried the whole evening long, until her cheeks were covered with a grey crust of salt. She realized that it would be a long time before Kare came home to them again. And in some way she was crying not just for Kare but also for Könik.

After that, Kare was gone every morning when she woke up. The box he had lain in was left where it was and she would go to it and hold on to the side of it to stop herself falling, and look down into it, but it was always empty. Könik never even dared look at it. Either Kare was alive or he wasn't. But he still had the figure that he'd carved and that hung on a thong around his neck. Each time Eira saw that he was still gone she always thought: Perhaps he'll come home today. No one will buy him, and the thief will give up in the end and return him. He's valueless, and yet the most valuable thing on earth. With that thought in her mind she was able to do everything that had to be done during the day.

But she started going to Ädla's and Bera's, not for any special reason and not even to talk for a while. She just sat there looking at the children.

One morning Eira saw something moving in the box: a rabbit

had made itself a nest there. That was the first time she killed a rabbit with her own hands.

Önde's sow, the mother sow who had given birth to Blasius, fell sick at about that time. All days and times now in Kadis were referred to as about that time. By saying that they could describe and handle time without giving it a name. They replaced particular and definite time with a time of the utmost generality. Not even Önde pretended to know the names of the days. In principle they could have borrowed a division of time from Umeå, names and numbers, just as you borrow fire from a neighbour, but what would have been the point of it now that things were the way they were with everything else? They quite simply didn't have any use for the counting of hours or days at about that time.

The sow, then, was no longer eating as she should, not even butter and cream. Mostly she just lay still on the straw and snored. But she didn't seem unhappy – no, she peered round through half-closed eyes absent-mindedly and almost contentedly, and lifted up her belly a little from time to time as if she wanted to invite all the little piglets she had borne over the years to come back and suckle again. Her flesh was shrinking like snow in the thaw, her skin was sagging and losing its glow the way it does with old people, her haunches and shoulders were withering as if they'd been dried over an open fire. And her face became more and more human, she began to look like an old woman who had seen generation after generation travel off into the dangerous world, wrinkled and full of wisdom. She'd lost her teeth long ago.

Önde watched over her till the end. And when she'd gone to sleep for good, he dragged her off on a sled and buried her behind the wall above the chapel.

He had come back from his trip up to the forest before all this happened with the sow. He'd been a long way. Ädla had to sit down straight away and mend his trousers that he'd torn on several seams, and he'd had to bind his shoes up with osiers.

But he'd come back almost empty-handed, just some bundles of birch bark and a bag of sundew and a few buzzards' eggs to feed Maria with. And a little piece of woollen cloth.

It wasn't especially remarkable cloth, it was woven by someone who didn't have much thread, thinly woven so that you could see through it, and coarse and uneven. He had come to an isolated house, a farm that until then had been unknown to the whole world and would probably remain unknown, since Önde had already forgotten where it was. He had taken pity on the people there and bought the cloth. He happened to have a silver coin in his money belt. And now it was his irrevocable decision that Eira should have this cloth.

"But what would they want with a silver coin out there in the wilds?" said Eira.

"Silver," said Önde, "that's still the only thing that's firm and lasting."

"Yes, but even so," said Eira.

"Everything else," said Önde, "we have because we've got to. But we have silver purely for pleasure."

Könik raised his head at this and looked at him, but said nothing and remained expressionless.

But why should Eira have this cloth, then?

Önde listed all the reasons he could think of.

She had taken on Blasius. She had had so many sorrows. Not to mention this latest one with Kare. She had bandaged up the wounds that a mad knife had once inflicted on him. She was so good to his and Avar's and Ädla's Maria. She had such patience. Yes, really he would rather have had her than Ädla. She was looking after Könik now that things were the way they were.

And to put an end to this heart-rending enumeration Eira finally accepted the cloth. She sometimes used it as a headscarf.

Blasius was now so big that there was no longer any point in wondering whether he was still growing. Indeed he was so gigantic that sometimes at night Eira would dream about his huge size – repugnant dreams – then when she came out to him in the morning it seemed to her that he'd shrunk. Borne thought that a pig couldn't get any bigger and still be a pig, that at a certain size he would cease to be a boar and become something else hitherto unknown; but Önde was convinced that Creation knew no bounds.

There was so little happening in Kadis that it really was worth taking note of whether Blasius was continuing to grow. It was a lack of events that couldn't be expressed in words. Avar's and Ädla's Maria started to stand up and walk, but beyond that nothing happened. And Bera, who was still suckling Jasper, was soon about to bear Borne another child.

And Ädla still refused to put herself at Önde's disposal for any conceiving or child-bearing.

Eira wanted to have a child to replace the stolen Kare – no, not to replace him, but a child to divert her while she waited for Kare to come back, a child in a general sense – but Könik refused. Or more precisely: he couldn't bring himself to do it, he would have had to set himself in motion so uncontrollably and dangerously that no one could know where it might lead. He wanted to lie alone in his bed by the wall, and he avoided looking at Eira, especially when she was washing herself or combing her hair or getting herself ready for the night.

Eira had once heard that people who went out of their minds could be cured. You had to kill an animal, a cat or a dog or whatever was to hand, and take out the intestines, and then tie the warm body over the head that was sick. And she tried: Könik went round for a whole day with a little bloody corpse tied to the top of his head. He looked as if he had two heads, his own and a rabbit's – two faces fixed in impotence and grief. Nothing happened. He got sore marks on his forehead and when he got into bed at night the rabbit fell off. But both Eira and Könik realized that he would never have gone along with such strange treatment if he'd been in full possession of his reason.

Some nights a creature came and sat astride him and rode him till he could hardly breathe.

A winter passed and it turned to spring again. The snow always thawed early in Kadis because it was on a south-facing slope. And they sowed the barley. And the turnips and cabbages too. They used only the best land. Osier bushes were already growing on the stoniest and most recently cleared fields. Even Könik dug a few patches of land and sowed seed, but Eira had to stay with him the whole time and remind him of what he was meant to be doing, otherwise he just stood there with his arms hanging by his side and his eyes half-closed.

Then one morning a stranger arrived. Könik was standing midway between the house and the carpenter's shop – he often stood there as if he was on his way to the one or the other, but really he wasn't on his way to anywhere. The man came the same way as Olavus the trader had once come. He had gone past Bera's house without going in; in fact it was impossible for him to know where any people could be found among all these empty houses. He had seen Könik.

He was not hurrying, he was examining the houses and the woodpiles and the frames where they used to dry their nets. Two rabbits were running along right in front of his feet. When he came up to Könik he took off his rucksack.

He asked whether he'd arrived in Kadis. He had a strong lisp, and it made his speech slow, in fact rather formal.

"Yes," said Könik. This was Kadis.

He had no beard, he was a head taller than any man Könik had seen before, and around his forehead he wore a band woven with silver threads.

"Then everything is as it should be," he said.

Könik said nothing, he'd never heard anything more absurd – that everything was as it should be.

"I am thirsty," the stranger added.

"You should go to Önde," said Könik. "We always send everyone to Önde."

"Don't you even have water?" the stranger asked.

Eira came out at that moment; she had heard the voices. She had her sleeves rolled up and her tunic hitched up because she'd been standing at the water tub rinsing fish that Önde had brought.

"We've got milk," she said. "And beer."

So the man went past Könik and into the house. And Eira poured out some milk for him.

"It's not often we see anyone, here in Kadis," she said.

That was her way of asking: What manner of man are you and what's your business?

Könik had followed them but stopped in the doorway. He held his hand over the ear he'd lost.

"We must send him to Önde," he said.

"He's thirsty," said Eira. "And he wants to sit down for a while. He might have been tramping and trudging along for ages."

When he'd drunk the milk he wanted to tell them who he was. His name was Nils. But when necessary he could be called Nikolavus.

"Strangers who come here always go to Önde," said Könik. "We send them to him."

But the stranger didn't listen to Könik. It was in fact not a matter of chance that he had ended up in Kadis, he had not walked at random and lost his way. No, he was on the King's business, he was an emissary.

162

Eira, who had gone back to rinsing the fish, stopped absolutely still at that, and Könik's hand dropped down from his ear and hung against his chest.

Neither Eira nor Könik could remember when the word king had last entered their thoughts. They had completely forgotten that there was or even could be a King. Once, a dreadfully long time ago, Kadis used to pay taxes to the King.

Yes, the King himself had sent him – and he even mentioned the King's name – he had sent him north as a scout and inspector. He, Nils, was to commit to memory all the buildings and people he encountered. He was to carry right on up country until he came to empty nothingness.

"Then you've arrived," said Könik.

What had happened was that something that was called the Great Sickness had swept over the earth like a carpenter's plane, in some places the people had been completely erased from the face of the earth, in others not a hair had been ruffled – yes, there were places where the Sickness had not even penetrated in the form of the word itself or the story of it, and the King needed to know now what people he still owned. So he had sent him, Nils. That's how things were.

"So you're one of the King's men," said Könik – and he didn't whisper but spoke very clearly and almost eagerly.

"As you say," said Nils, the stranger.

At that Könik came forward and sat down on the stool opposite him. He rested his elbows on his knees and looked at him.

"The King," said Könik, "he doesn't send out just anyone."

And now Nils explained that he certainly wasn't just anyone. He had served the Crown for many years. Well, served probably wasn't the best word: he had become an integral part of it. Serving in this case was often synonymous with being master; there was of course only one King, but the people's need of royalty is insatiable, so anyone who served the Crown often had quite simply to act as the Crown. He had to assume an inner, invisible crown, and bring order and justice where injustice and disorder and confusion had got the upper hand. And for that reason the servants of the Crown were selected with great care. In his own case he had studied law and the true belief and the theory of peoples and kings in the biggest cities in the world, in cities with such names as Cologne and Paris and Bologna, in cities that could have the strangest names imaginable, and he had trained in all the things that might be called the arts of the Crown with foreign lords in other countries. The fact that he was now in Kadis he himself would rather regard as a somewhat comical turn of events.

And he burst into a short, rasping laugh.

Then all was silent.

But Eira looked at Könik: something was happening to his face. And he bent forward towards this Nils as if to reassure himself he was not just an illusion, as if he was trying to identify his odour. Finally she said: "It's to Önde you should go."

What was happening to Könik's face was that the furrow was deepening and darkening, it was becoming a great cleft between the two halves of his forehead. And his cheeks and lips and eyes were no longer still and immobile. One half of his face was trembling with grief and despair, the other was smooth and clear – yes, almost shining with hope and expectation. Eira became strangely uneasy and distressed when she saw what was happening to him – she had got used to his being stiff and numb – and she repeated: "Really it's Önde you should go to."

But Könik said: "Önde. No, he's got nothing to do with this."

"Who is Önde?" Nils asked.

Eira and Könik were both silent at that. It was a question they'd never worried about before.

So a person had come who really knew how things should be, who recognized what was fitting and proper, who could distinguish right from wrong.

"You've really sat in judgement?" Könik asked in hope, yet with some distrust.

"Over people and animals, property and chattels," said Nils.

164

"It's not the King who's sent you," said Könik. "It's God."

Now Nils looked at Könik more critically than before, and his eyes focused on the ear that was missing.

"My task is only to count you," he said suspiciously. "Nothing more."

But everything that Könik had pushed down into the darkness deep within himself, everything that he'd tried to salt away in his flesh, now rose up in him, the disorder and confusion and injustice, it filled his breast so that he was forced to straighten up and put his hands behind his back.

First of all he had to say what had happened to his ear.

"This ear," he said, "wasn't my fault. It was a knife that once broke loose. The knife did it of its own accord."

And the man called Nils said nothing. He had heard many earless men explain themselves.

But then Könik was compelled to speak about the hardest thing of all, the confusion that made life impossible to live, the darkness and disorder from which they all needed to be delivered.

"We've got a pig," he said. "It's a boar and he's absurdly large. If everything were as it should be, a pig wouldn't be able to reach that size."

When Eira had finished rinsing the fish she put it in the pot and poured in two ladles of water and blew life into the embers.

"A pig," said Nils.

"Yes. A pig. He's called Blasius."

"Blasius," said Nils, "was a holy bishop who fled to a cave to escape his persecutors. Wolves and foxes and rabbits brought food to him secretly. When his pursuers found him and killed him the lake to which they dragged him was turned into dry land. He cures coughs and quinsy and spiritual ailments."

"If you see him," said Könik, "you'll understand."

And Nils got up and went to the sty with Könik. There was Blasius, surrounded by rabbits. He was now as tall as the railing. When they arrived he sat on his haunches, put his head on one side and shook his collar and bell just as he used to when Eira came with the food.

"There he is," said Könik.

And Nils admitted it: he had never seen a pig like that nor anything remotely resembling it. He wished that he could take Blasius to the south and show him to the King.

"Once," said Könik, "he was even luminous."

Blasius grunted and waved to them with his front legs. A frightened rabbit tried to hide under his sex organ that was resting on the straw in front of him.

"Someone must have mercy on us in the end and pass judgement on all this," said Könik. He had tears in his eyes now.

"Judgement," said Nils.

"Yes," said Könik. "If no one will judge us and what has befallen us, we will sink deeper and deeper into absurdity and perdition."

"You have plenty of rabbits here in Kadis," said Nils, changing the subject.

But the rabbits were also part of what Könik wanted him to know about and understand – yes, the rabbits mirrored in their lives the situation prevailing in Kadis. He might as well begin his account with the rabbits as with anything else.

Rabbits and sickness and death. Avar and Ädla. And Olavus the trader. Property that no one owned, and inheritances. The chapel that was deserted and the beasts they had killed. Yes, he spoke about everything that has been told here and much more besides, because of course he had lived through it all himself. And time, the reckoning of time that had been forgotten, the days that came and went without anyone calling them by name.

"That which doesn't have a name," said Könik, "doesn't exist."

"Today is Saint Romuald's Day," said Nils.

Könik was silent for a moment. He would remember that for ever: Saint Romuald's Day.

But then he went on. No one was certain of anything any more, no one had any knowledge. If the crescent moon is like

166

a bowl, will it be dry or rainy? Everything that was worth knowing had been buried with the dead. How do you make a net so that it comes out right? How do you weld iron? What do you do with people who steal silver from the living and the dead? And people who have sex with cows? Not to mention a man who tries to kill his dearest friend with a knife. Even if the friend is a desecrator of graves and a plunderer of corpses.

"I know nothing," said Nils, "about the right way to make a net."

"And a plunderer of corpses and a desecrator of graves," Könik went on, "should he be hanged? And a person who has appropriated anvil and tongs from a dead smith? And a woman who flaunts stolen silver round her neck? And children begotten by their fathers in their daughters, should they live?"

Nils with the silver-threaded band round his head stood there in front of this unbelievable pig listening and trying to understand. Könik had a peculiar way of talking all his own, eagerly and expectantly but at the same time in tears.

"I can see," said Nils, "that you have suffered here in Kadis from disorder beyond all comprehension."

"Yes," said Könik.

"But this pig, which is probably the most magnificent in the kingdom – what has it to do with the matter?"

"Blasius," said Könik, "has in one sense the body of a pig. But in reality he's a sign and a symbol. He represents something beyond himself."

Blasius had lain down, he was no longer interested in these two empty-handed men.

"And what does he represent?" asked Nils.

"Unrestrained excess," said Könik. "A situation without rules or standards."

Nils had seen countless oddities in towns with the strangest names. He looked at Blasius now – two rabbits had settled down on him, and their almost non-existent weight caused softly-rounded hollows in the flesh of his side.

"What you need is a priest," he said at last.

"That's what I told you," said Könik. "We had a priest, but he was among the first to die."

"You must get a new one. We'll have to send a message to the Bishop."

"Who will take the message?" Könik asked.

"One of you."

"Ädla has to look after Maria," said Könik. "Önde is needed with Ädla. And he would steal the Bishop's holy gold ring. We can't send Borne on such a mission. Bera has to suckle Jasper. I can't go, I keep losing my reason off and on. And Eira has to be here at home keeping an eye on me."

Now Blasius had snapped up one of the rabbits. He hardly even had to chew it. Nils thought for a long time, then he said: "I shall tell everything to the King."

"What good will that do us?" Könik asked. "Telling a crazy and preposterous tall story to the King."

"A tall story?" said Nils.

"Yes," said Könik. "Because that's what it is."

"If only I could," said Nils, "I'd help you."

"You said yourself," said Könik, "that you've learned all about justice. In towns with the strangest names. That you know everything there is to know about justice."

"Justice," said Nils, "that's only a concept. It needs laws and judges and clerks in order to work."

"You can be the law and its clerk and the judge," said Könik.

Nils stroked his smoothly shaven chin. Könik would come to notice that eventually: every time he weighed up the many different possibilities and solutions he stroked his chin with the palm of his left hand.

"It is clear," he said, looking now neither at Blasius nor at Könik but staring straight down at the ground, "that I could judge in one afternoon the things you have told me about. I could decide these minor matters between the midday meal and Vespers."

"There's not that much of a hurry," said Könik, "we have all the time in the world. Or rather, in Kadis we have no time at all."

"In a few days' time," said Nils, "it will be John the Baptist's Day."

"Oh," said Könik. That was also something he would remember for ever, John the Baptist's Day.

"But," Nils went on, "how would that help you? If you were condemned for one thing or another that you've done here in this confusion and isolation? If I took the time to put on trial those of you who need it? And if I issued a handful of judgements?"

"In the King's name," said Könik.

"Of course," said Nils. "In the King's name."

Könik stretched himself up now as much as he could and raised his face towards him. Half of his face was hard and strong, half was humbly begging. The scar where his ear had been was glowing dark red.

"We would get light and clarity," he said. "A new Kadis. We could build everything again from nothing. First the judgement and then a new life."

"And who would carry out my and the King's judgements?"

"Borne," said Könik. "Borne was hangman here in Kadis before the Sickness stirred us up like a pig stirs its pig-swill in the trough."

"You're a remarkable man," said Nils. "You say that you lose your reason from time to time?"

"I was rational all the time before," said Könik.

"But now?" said Nils.

"Right now," said Könik, "I've got my reason."

"You're certain of that?" said Nils.

"Never since the rabbits came to Kadis have I been in possession of my reason so surely as I am now."

"I know many people," said Nils, "who would count themselves blessed if there were no order and nobody judged them."

And Könik said the only sensible thing he could say: "They have never experienced injustice and confusion."

But now Eira came out. She had been going to call them, but thought better of it. She came up to them and curtseyed to Nils – yes, she really curtseyed, and said that the fish was cooked, not just cooked, she said, it had started to break apart. So they went in and ate. She'd put out the fish in the glazed clay dish – never before had a man of the Crown eaten under her roof – and she'd cut up the bread with a knife.

She told him about Kare, the son they had had stolen. That really was something to be surprised about: Könik hadn't mentioned a single word about Kare, they'd stood out there with Blasius talking for a long time, but he hadn't remembered to say even in passing that as well as Eira and Blasius he also had a son, or at least had had a son.

"Yes, of course," he said now. "Someone came and stole him one night. But you have to be prepared for that sort of thing."

And he held out the little wooden head that was hanging round his neck.

"A well-formed child," said Nils.

"I carved it to have a remembrance of him," said Könik.

And Eira didn't remind him that when he carved that image they still had Kare with them.

Nils took the fish away from his mouth but said nothing for a while. He had sucked the bone almost clean so that only the skeleton remained. He pondered in sympathy the lost son and the fish.

"I heard about that," he said. "When the Sickness was raging at its worst and births couldn't keep up with deaths, a child could change owners ten times a day."

"Yes," said Könik.

"But now," he went on, "now those times are long past."

"Here in Kadis," said Könik, "it's hard to know what times are past."

"It was just a blind lust to bear fruit. No one gave themselves time to conceive and give birth. Frenzy and feverish madness and nothing more."

"But he will come back," said Eira.

"Everything returns," said Nils. "Everything reverts to its origins. There is a time for breaking up and a time for dispersing, but also a time for returning and coming back."

"He's only away for a short time, getting to know the world," said Eira. "But this is where his home is."

"Restoration," said Nils, "is the main rule of life. Separation is the exception. Most of the time life is concerned with restoring itself."

"Are you talking about Kare now?" Könik asked.

"Of course," said Nils. "He is included in what I'm saying."

But his gaze was moving round the room without fixing on anything, and he couldn't look at Eira or Könik.

"I learned that in far-off foreign cities. The doctrine of law and the doctrine of God both have that in common. Restoration."

Then they all fell silent. He was still holding the fish in his fingers. None of them knew what to say next. Though Eira said: "The fish is whitefish." But within herself she felt something almost like joy, a dark yet also very bright sense of consolation from the grand and incomprehensibly deep meaning that this man Nils had attributed to her Kare and his disappearance and certain return.

And Könik said: "Sometimes at night a creature comes and sits astride me, setting its feet each side of my hips, then riding me so madly that I can't breathe and I feel as if I've been beaten black and blue."

And thus Nils – or should he now be called Nikolavus? – learned that Könik had been ridden by a hag or succubus.

Nothing more was said about his going to Önde. Why had Könik taken the trouble to build a room on to the house if the room couldn't be used at a time like this by a man of the Crown with silver threads in his headband?

171

Eira brought in the straw and made a bed for him on the seat that Könik had made along the wall. And Nils and Könik went out to look around Kadis. They didn't go into anyone's house and they didn't meet anyone. They saw the water gully where the water was yellow even though it was the middle of the summer. They saw all the barred and shuttered houses. And all Önde's marks. And the half-rotted fence that was called, or had been called, the wall. And the ground that was still black and dead where they had burned the animals. It was a light night. They saw countless numbers of rabbits.

"A magnificent place," said Nils. "A superb place."

They went into the chapel. Önde had stored a pile of last year's hay there in front of the big cross. Könik showed Nils the figure he had carved, the one that resembled Önde however you looked at it.

"Yes," Nils lisped, "piety and a love of truth certainly radiate from that face – yes, from its whole body. Is it James the Apostle? Or perhaps Joseph the Stepfather?"

"I'm not really sure," said Könik. "It might be just about anyone."

And finally they went to bed in Könik's house. Nils took his rucksack with him into the new room that was the only real room in Kadis. Könik couldn't sleep. Even though his eyelids were closed the night light from the window apertures penetrated to his eyes. It was like the light that Eira had once produced by rubbing the furrow that divided his face in two.

Eira came to bed last of all. She always had to take food to Blasius before she could sleep so that he would survive the night.

The next morning Könik said to Nils: "It would be best if you stay in the house today. You can never be sure here in Kadis, it's not wise to go around as a stranger – one of us might kill you by mistake."

So Nils lay on his bed when he wasn't eating with Eira. He lay looking up at the ceiling, where the pine timber was still new, and out through the smoke aperture – the day was sunny and clear. He lay thinking about everything that Könik had told him, and rearranged the jumble of small everyday events into a more coherent, perhaps even usable and useful, form. A doe rabbit with a belly full of young had come over to him: she lay on his chest and he stroked her back. He was working things out and putting them together – many things remained obscure and confused. But something resembling a general understanding or a story nevertheless began to emerge. He ran his fingers through the rabbit's fur, which was so soft that at moments his fingertips almost doubted the rabbit's existence. And he attributed the beginning of everything to a doe rabbit that a young man on his way home from Nordingrå had brought with him from Umeå to Kadis. If he got out of here alive he didn't want to go empty-handed, he wanted to have a story to tell. So more or less everything we know about Kadis we have originally from him.

Könik went to see Önde. He was sitting with Maria on his lap and giving her dried blueberries that he was holding in his hand. He was putting them on her outstretched tongue one at a time. Maria was now at an age when she tottered about heedlessly all over the place; she had learned to walk but still didn't understand what was said to her. Somebody had to be with her all the time, otherwise she might wander off right into the fire or disappear into the forest.

Önde realized immediately that Könik had some news to impart. He couldn't remember when he'd last seen Könik's eyes and lips really open and move. He lifted Maria over to Ädla's lap and tossed the remaining blueberries into his own mouth.

They went out and stood in the shade behind Avar's old rowan tree where no one could hear them.

"I've got a man of the Crown at my house," said Könik.

"I know," said Önde.

"How can you know?"

"The whole of Kadis knows."

"He's a fearfully strict and stern man," said Könik. "He's ruling my household like the devil himself."

"And he's really a man of the Crown?" said Önde.

"He's got a letter with the King's stamp on. And the King's ring on his finger."

"But what does he want?" asked Önde.

"If only I really knew," said Könik. "But he's not the sort of man you can make out straight away."

"You'd better send him to me," said Önde.

"I've said that. I've said: 'It's usual for all strangers to go to Önde.' But he says he's not going to leave my house until he's done what he's come to do."

"But what is it, then, that he has to do?"

"He's come to put us on trial. He's going to question us and judge us."

"He's lost his senses," said Önde.

"He will himself be the law and the clerk of the court and the judge. He will restore and reinstate everything and give us clarity and light."

"Is that really what he says?"

"Yes," said Könik. "Word for word. And he lisps."

"Well, there you are," said Önde. "He's not reliable."

174

"He's from the south, where people have a grander way of talking," said Könik.

"We've never done anything wrong," said Önde.

"That's what I told him," said Könik. "But he just says that the King has sent him."

"And we're supposed to believe that?" said Önde. "That the King has sent an envoy to Kadis?"

"He's sent him all over the place," said Könik. "What he's doing here, he's doing everywhere he goes."

Önde pondered this for a while, and without thinking what he was doing he carved his mark of ownership on Avar's old rowan tree, two deep notches with a shallow cut across them. Then he said: "We must take him and kill him."

"You can't kill a King's man," said Könik. "If you kill a King's man, there'll be ten more come looking for him."

Önde gave a heavy, tired sigh.

"And things were so quiet and good here," he said. "For us who live at peace with the whole of Creation and the universe."

"Yes," said Könik.

"And you're sure about him being here in the King's name?"

"He says it himself," said Könik. "In the King's name. And he wants to set things up in the chapel. You'll have to take last year's hay out."

So it was just as well to go along with it and get the annoyance over and done with, to go through the investigation and get rid of this man Nils, this King's man or whatever he was, so that he could go on to somewhere else – anywhere else.

Önde went to Borne; Könik went home.

"Everything is prepared and ready now," he said to Nils, who was lying fully dressed on the bed.

"For what?"

"For the trial you're going to conduct."

"If I had foreseen what you would demand of me here in Kadis," said Nils, "I would have gone back to the King and said that the world ended at Umeå."

175

"That might well have been true," said Könik.

"The whole thing is a cruel trick," said Nils.

"Here in Kadis," said Könik, "it's impossible to make a distinction between a trick and the seriousness of death."

Nils sat up and looked at Könik thoughtfully, but he was also smiling. He looked suddenly as if what he was about to experience in Kadis had livened him up.

"Yes," he said, "real, profound tricks are so serious that we can thank our Maker if we escape with our lives."

"You should have a ring on your finger," said Könik.

Nils picked up his rucksack and opened it. It rattled when he put his hand in it, and there was a clinking of metal. Soon he had not one but four rings on his fingers, two on each hand.

"Which is the King's?" Könik asked.

"It could well be all four," said Nils. "The King isn't so particular about his rings, he hands them out the way you scatter crumbs for the birds."

"If only you had a robe," said Könik.

"I could go on my way," said Nils. "And leave you all to your fate. I'm not an actor or a conjuror."

But even as he spoke he put his hand down into his rucksack again. And this time he found a robe or cloak. The cloth was so fine that when rolled up it fitted into the palm of his hand. He shook it out in front of him and draped it over his shoulders. He was obviously prepared for everything.

"Yes," said Könik. "Now we can see that you're a man of the Crown."

The robe was black and shiny and had a white cross on the back. Eira came and admired it. It was strangely moving to see that clean-shaven face against the black cloth. She had never seen a clean-shaven face before.

But Önde had gone to Borne's and said: "Könik has talked that stranger into setting up some kind of court; he's going to investigate and judge everything that's happened here in Kadis since the rabbits came."

"Bera says that he's a man of the Crown," said Borne.

"Yes," said Önde.

"So is it serious then, or a trick?" said Borne.

"It would be you who asks something like that," said Önde. "If you can explain to me how we can tell the difference between tricks and seriousness, I'll give you a piece of silver as big as your fist."

And so Önde went off. But Borne stood there pondering and looking in disbelief at his enormous fist.

*Mere Trifles*

N evertheless that was the first thing that was said when they gathered in the chapel. It was Borne who asked: "Is this meant to be a trick or is it serious?"

But this question was even more absurd now than when he had put it to Önde.

Nikolavus explained calmly and still with a slight lisp that here before the judge, in the Court, while it was in session, you only spoke in a fixed order, when it was your duty to speak, and only if it was necessary to do so.

Nikolavus sat in the high seat that Könik had made for the priest a fearfully long time ago.

The people – that is, Önde and Könik and Borne – sat before him on a log they had put across two blocks. Their beards were streaked with their midday food.

The women were standing down by the door. Bera's goats were bleating outside and their little bells were tinkling. The rabbits that had lived undisturbed in the chapel for so long were running hither and thither in fright. Yes, the whole of Kadis was there.

When they used to gather in the chapel before the Sickness and the rabbits came, the adults had often lifted the children up on to their shoulders so that they wouldn't get trampled in the crush.

Könik remembered that he'd once anxiously put Eira on his shoulders. They'd been standing so close together that they'd all been leaning against one another. It had been impossible to know who was really standing upright and who was just being supported by the others.

The whole of Kadis.

Now Nikolavus was going to continue the story that Könik had started telling him.

He began to speak.

He just wanted to introduce the proceedings, he said. The day was already well advanced – the following day, on the other hand, could be expected to be a day of judgement.

Though of course he had no idea of what the next day would bring.

"The law," he continued, "is to defend the defenceless and give peace to the peaceable, but to punish the violent and bring the wicked and the foolish to the truth. If everyone acted in accordance with the law, there would be no need for the law.

"Where there is justice, the water runs clear in the gully, the days are named and numbered, the dead lie at rest in their graves, children are conceived in the right and proper way, and fish nets are made in the correct manner."

He was not lisping, and he was speaking loudly and slowly as if he had a large crowd of people before him. The rabbits hid in their burrows in the earth of the floor.

"If there are nettles, thistles and thorns growing among noble fruit," he said, "they have to be uprooted and thrown away. God grant that we all may live according to the law, that we all may attain the kingdom of heaven, and that we all may so live with our brothers that we receive the mercy of heaven."

And Könik and Önde and Borne and Eira and Ädla and Bera were struck dumb. Not even the priest had spoken so forcefully and movingly. They didn't need to hear many words to realize that he held the whole of Kadis in his power. Man and beast and property and chattels. And the rabbits. He spoke solemnly, exactly as the original Jasper had done when he had explained the nature of rabbits to them and begun his preposterous story.

He also had to deplore the fact that attendance at this Court, at this solemn occasion, was so poor. He presumed that those who were not present had lawful reason to stay away. Since, however, they were so few, he must impress upon them the importance and necessity for them all to strive their utmost to disclose as much of the truth as possible, so that justice could be meted out upon all those who had rendered themselves deserving of it. From time to time in his speech he also reminded them that he was acting in the name of the King, and he raised his fingers so that all four rings were visible; there were silver chains around his wrists that chinked like little bells. No one should think that law and justice – to the extent to which one could here speak of the law – were a trick, except in so far as all law and order was fundamentally a great practical joke with which God made fun of his poor, wretched Creation, and justice was simply a pastime for God on the eighth day. But he would leave that aside. No, all those gathered here today must carry out their obligations with the courage of their desperation and in cheerful trust, as plaintiffs and defendants and also as lay-judges. They must let the roles of plaintiff and defendant and judge so mingle together that they no longer knew which was which – only thus could the way be prepared for assigning guilt or setting free or sentencing.

And in passing he described the punishment for a dishonest lay-judge: His hands were to be bound, a cloth placed over his eyes, he would be thrown down on his stomach and his tongue pulled round to the back of his head. Then a strong rope would be placed about his neck and he would be hanged seven feet higher than an outlawed thief.

Borne leaned forward and tilted his head on one side to be able to hear better. He hadn't heard that bit about pulling out the tongue to the back of the head before. Nikolavus was getting hot from all this speaking. He lifted a corner of his black robe and dried his forehead. From time to time as he sought a particularly elusive or splendid word he would rub his chin with the palm of his left hand.

He sincerely regretted that the pursuit of order and justice would demand that questions be put, questions they would find painful but which they must nevertheless strive to answer honestly. But they were not to despair about these questions, such questions as whether anyone had absent-mindedly or thoughtlessly borrowed jewellery from the graves of the dead, or had had over-affectionate dealings with a cow, or carved his sign by mistake into some piece of wood that looked prettier without a sign. Those questions would only be put if nothing unforeseen happened, but the unforeseen often happened, despite everything.

He said this as if he already knew what would happen.

And here, of course, it was not in the first instance a case of any one individual pursuing his rights, not a single injured party bitterly or aggressively identifying and accusing a fellow-creature and demanding his blood. No, here it was a case of a more general and abstract search for law and order, justice as a fundamental principle or invisible concept or illusion or state – yes, state was probably the best word, a state that might be likened to satiation or sleep or intoxication, a comical intoxication as from strong beer, a sense of spiritual well-being bordering on the shameful, law and order as a source of joy and as a stimulating drink and solace for oppressed souls. One might also say that what they were seeking here was the natural order, something only dimly perceived but which would appear self-evident and irrefutable everywhere and always. Possibly he should in this context raise a warning, half-regal, finger: law and order are like fire – once it has caught hold it is difficult to stop, it consumes everything in its path, and finally it consumes itself.

Borne was supporting his head on his hands now and sleeping. Önde's knife was carving owner's marks in bewilderment one after another in the log they were sitting on. One half of Könik's face was smiling at the beauty of the words, the other half was grimly furrowed at their meaning.

Yes, there was no end to what could be said about law and order. Ultimately, he pointed out, it was sickness and death that should be held responsible – yes, everywhere that men lived and dwelt sickness and death should be held responsible, since it was these two, in reality forming one single entity, that had appropriated and distorted all permanent and natural states. But we were powerless against such over-lords even if we came in the name of the King. He spoke great quantities of words which seemed to come from the obscure depths of his memory and which were meant to be reminiscent of knowledge from foreign cities with the strangest names. No one understood what he said, and he did not commit it to memory himself, so it is not recorded even here.

Finally, before they completed their deliberations for the day and went off to their night's rest, he wanted to let peace reign over Kadis, in the King's name. From now on and for as long as there was uncertainty about anything at all, everything should be left as it was, nothing should be dug up or buried, no owner's marks should be cut, no objects moved from their rightful place, no lusts of the flesh gratified in unsuitable ways. "Peace be with you all."

Könik and Önde and Borne rose silently and carefully as if they'd been to Holy Mass with the priest. The goats were silent outside. The rabbits were nowhere to be seen – it was doubtful whether they would ever show themselves in Kadis again. Ädla and Eira and Bera, who had been standing down by the door, could no longer feel their legs, they had gone numb from all this earnest and devout standing. They had stood there the whole time except for the short while when they ran home and did the evening milking. Bera had Jasper in his basket, Ädla had Maria in her arms.

Nikolavus took Borne to one side. For the continuation of this performance a wooden scaffold was needed, in a very visible place. He wanted Borne to build this scaffold, for it was Borne, was it not, who was called the hangman here in Kadis? A scaffold that could be used for any purpose but that could not be mis-understood. Two thick poles and a cross-bar.

185

"We used to have one," said Borne, "but it rotted in the ground and fell down."

He, Borne, would not go unrewarded, he could be sure of rings and bracelets as well as pieces of silver if he assisted with sober dignity and appropriate care in this grim jest and laughably serious business.

"I won't take anything," said Borne. "I'm just doing my duty for Kadis."

Eira tried to talk to Könik on the way home. Why had he really arranged these distressing proceedings or practical joke or whatever it was, why had he persuaded this King's man Nils, whom they now had to call Nikolavus, to stay – yes, not just to stay but to set himself over them and upon them? But Könik was silent. Never had he imagined that light and clarity were so incomprehensible and confused, so ridiculous and threatening. He was partly pleased, but on the whole he was in deep despair. "I don't understand anything," he said.

"Is it because of Kare?" Eira asked. "You shouldn't worry yourself about Kare. It's only a short while, and he'll soon be home again."

"I'm sure of that," she added.

"Before," said Könik, "I was always sure why I did one thing or another."

"We should always be aware of what we do," said Eira. "We should never do anything that we don't understand ourselves."

Yes, she even raised her voice and shouted at him in a way she had never done before:

"We shouldn't be like sleepwalkers, if we make ourselves blind and deaf we'll fall into every single pit – yes, into every chasm there is. If you'd only known what you were doing, no evil would ever have befallen us."

When they got home they had their evening meal. Nikolavus came and ate with them too. He sat over by the fire and cut his own food and ate. Eira and Könik sat on their beds and chewed their crusts of bread and their dried rabbit meat.

"The rabbit tastes sweet," said Nikolavus. "But it fills you up for a long time."

Eira and Könik said nothing.

And then it was time to bed down for the night. Nikolavus was always tired in the evenings. It was a habit you acquired in the service of the King – everyone had to go to first Mass in the morning and so had to use the evening and the night for sleep.

Könik and Nikolavus went to their beds. Eira had to mix the pig-food and feed Blasius.

Könik fell asleep almost immediately. But Nikolavus lay awake for a while. He had heard Eira lifting buckets and bowls and working with ladles and knives. He lay thinking about this story of Kadis that he had now made his own and how he was going to finish it, how slowly it had advanced till now and how easily he, had appropriated everything, and what pleasure it gave him to be able to make anything at all happen from now on. He was the most remarkable man ever in Kadis, he was infused with the warmth of an uplifting and arrogant joy, and when the sounds of Eira's work ceased, he fell asleep.

But Eira put down the bucket of pig-food. She was tired too. She wanted to rest and gather her breath before she went in to Blasius. Könik was in a deep sleep, opening his mouth with a snore from time to time. Nikolavus was also asleep. He was breathing so gently and delicately that she had to put her hand behind her ear to hear him at all. His sleep was so refined that there wasn't even a hiss of air from his nostrils. And she thought she would go into the room where he was lying and look at him.

He had taken off the band that he always wore round his forehead. The evening sun shone on him through the aperture in the far wall. It was a reddish yellow light that made his hair shimmer and look almost translucent. It lay spread out like combed flax over the shirt that he had rolled up as a pillow beneath his head. That creasing of the skin around his eyes, the little wrinkles that prevented you from seeing whether he was joking or serious when he was awake, all had gone. It looked just as if he had completely surrendered his doubts and his jocularity now that he was asleep.

That morning he had shaved his chin and cheeks with a special knife that he kept in a leather pouch in his rucksack, then he had sweated quite a lot as he spoke in the chapel, and now he gleamed as if he had rubbed himself with lard. His face was naked and exposed, and Eira was embarrassed when she saw it. He had no cover over him, and nothing else on either. He had taken off the attire that made him a King's man, but the evening sun shining in from outside and his nakedness clothed him in a different kind of nobility and splendour. He lay outstretched with his arms at his side. He still had the four rings on his fingers and the silver chains round his wrists.

Eira didn't hear Blasius ringing his bell and calling for her.

He had hair, or rather, down, on his chest and legs, like a young rabbit a few weeks old. It was so soft and fine that it moved and quivered when she came near and breathed on it. He had little pearls of sweat on his neck and in the hollow of his navel. His mouth was not quite closed and he felt the inside of his lips with his tongue from time to time as if he wanted to lick up the last taste of something pleasant he had eaten. And his penis was stiff and pointing upwards, and as he breathed it swayed like a little tree standing alone in the wind.

When he had been in Umeå – yes, even in Nordingrå – he had intended to go to a woman. But he had forgotten. He just hadn't thought of it. But now in his sleep he was thinking of it.

He dreamed that he was lying resting. Before he lay down he had drunk a sweet wine and the taste was still on his lips. He was alone in an unknown and yet familiar place far in the north where the world ends. He could make anything happen that he wanted to. It was warm, and he was naked. Then a woman came, he dreamed, and she stopped and looked down upon him. He couldn't see that she was inspecting him because he was dreaming that he didn't want to open his eyes and reveal that he was awake, but he could feel it like an itching or tickling on his skin. She was touching and stroking him with her eyes. And he let his penis rise, it seemed an appropriate and pleasant thing to do. Then he dreamed that the woman lifted up her skirts and climbed up on to him in the bed. She put her legs each side of him with her ankles pressing against his hips, her right ankle against his left hip and her left against his right. Then she bent down and took his penis into herself, she let it into her so naturally and humbly that he didn't feel anything until it had already happened.

It was Eira who was doing it. She didn't know she was doing it, she was utterly innocent and as if blind and deaf or like a sleepwalker, she knew nothing at all of her actions. She was not doing it herself, it was simply being done.

And she had completely forgotten Blasius. She didn't hear him even though he was screaming now in the greatest anxiety. He himself thought that the whole of Kadis ought to wake up and come rushing with all the bowls and buckets there were, and he swung and banged the bell he had around his neck so that it sounded like a smith hammering on an anvil. His hunger was hardly life-threatening yet, but without his evening meal he did not believe he would survive the night.

So Eira was as if asleep and he received her in his sleep. It was indeed questionable whether what they were doing took place at all. After a while her movements became faster and more violent, she bumped up and down on him so that his pelvis and hips began to ache, and for a while his dream became blurred and confused, he felt it only in his body and not in his mind. But then it cleared again, and now she was no longer the woman who had come and looked so warmly and wonderingly upon him, but a creature riding him, a merciless creature who had taken over one of the parts of his body and was intent on wearing him away to nothing. And he dreamed that he must heave her off, he must throw her off his body and off the bed before she mangled him to shreds. But he couldn't move an inch, his fingers and arms and legs wouldn't obey him, he was as if paralyzed. Finally she was torturing him so unbearably that he tried to scream or at least wail or groan so that someone would hear him and come to his rescue or so that she would be persuaded to spare his life – but he couldn't manage even that.

But then Könik called from the house. "Eira," he called. "Eira."

She stopped quite still. And then she raised herself up from Nikolavus and let her skirts drop down and cover her again, and she climbed down from his bed as carefully and delicately as she had come. But her thoughts were still entirely benumbed and she moved as if in a trance. Only when she felt the cold earth floor beneath the soles of her feet did she begin to come to herself again. She stood for a moment wondering what she was actually doing in there. Nikolavus lay sleeping and he was naked. She remembered that she had been on her way out to Blasius with his evening meal and she thought she had just heard Könik calling her.

So she went back to Könik and to the bucket of pig-food.

"If only I knew what's got into Blasius," said Könik.

Blasius had created such a terrible din that Könik had woken up, although he slept so deeply that he didn't even have any dreams. They were silent for a moment and listened for him, but there was nothing to be heard any longer. There might be the tinkling of a bell somewhere, but it was so far away that it couldn't possibly be Blasius.

Nikolavus too was on the point of coming round. But what he had been through was so frightening and incomprehensible that he didn't have the strength to come properly to his senses. Half awake and half asleep he sat up and inspected his body. And it was unquestionably true that a hag had ridden him: his stomach and hips were swollen and inflamed and red, and he thought his penis looked like a newly-pulled rabbitskin turned inside out.

No, it was impossible for him to wake up properly. He lay down on his back and went to sleep again. He didn't even get involved in any new dreams. And then he didn't wake up until much later when Könik came in and called his name and asked a preposterous question, at the same time holding up and showing him something in his hand that was even more absurd.

Never before had Blasius had to wait so long for his evening meal. If it was waiting – waiting is what you do if something is certain to come in the end, like Eira waiting for Kare. No, what he was feeling was distress and consternation and bitterness. He had heard the old familiar clatter of pans and buckets from inside the house, and he had heard the knife hacking and the ladle pouring. He knew that Eira had done what she had to do up to that point and that the food was now ready in the bucket. He had heard turnips and carrots being lifted out of the pot and chopped up, and fish guts being scraped off the board, and groats being stirred in water. And he'd heard a little basin of sour milk being poured into the bucket. And he'd been able to hear everything being mixed and pounded. And he'd rung his bell in agreement and encouragement. But then everything had gone so strangely quiet. He could catch the sound of careful padding feet but nothing else, so he decided to send Eira a squeal of confirmation and exhortation, a reminder of her duties and his rights. He listened again. But all was silent. Or more correctly: all the sounds that reached him were irrelevant and insignificant. So he raised his voice and didn't just squeal but howled and roared as loud as his lungs and throat were able – yes, he caused a din that must have been heard over the whole of Kadis and that could have awoken the dead. And he'd swung his bell so hard that the collar had been thrown round and round his neck and the clapper nearly torn from its fastening. But no Eira and no bucket.

Then a great feeling of fear and desperation came upon him. The whole of Kadis – yes, probably the whole universe – must have become like this.

It was disorder beyond all comprehension, a situation without rules or guidelines. No one knew anything any longer, everything that was right and proper had been obliterated, the reckonings of time had been forgotten, not only evening meal time but probably morning meal and midday meal and water-filling and patting and scrubbing and grunting-with-him times as well. In his heart of hearts he had known for a long time that this would happen, that there would finally come an evening of absolute and excruciating and ultimate hunger and pointless and desolate cries out into empty nothingness. Now here he sat on his haunches, beating and flailing helplessly with his front legs. All he could feel was a confusion that made life impossible to live. If he stayed here he would sink deeper and deeper into absurdity and perdition. It was a state of darkness and disorder that he must save himself from.

In his distress and consternation and bitterness he threw himself with all his weight against the fence which till now had closed him in and given him all his comfort and security in the world. He no longer had any idea of what he was doing, it was as if he was blind and deaf, and the palings split and collapsed like rotten brushwood.

And so he plunged out into Kadis.

He didn't really know what he wanted or what he was looking for. He gave shrill and agitated squeals at intervals and his bell rang violently and clamorously in time with his running, and he rushed forward headlong as if in his sleep.

And he found nothing that made it worthwhile stopping. It would have to be something astounding and exquisite for him to stop, something that would arouse his attention despite his high speed and despite the fact that his thoughts and senses were fuddled and benumbed.

Everyone in Kadis heard him. Bera's goats began to scream and bleat in fear. And Bera, who was sitting with Jasper at her breast, said to Borne: "It's dreadful what Blasius is re-living tonight."

But Borne had no time to think about Blasius. "I must make a new scaffold," he said. "I wonder if Könik could help me."

Ädla and Önde were eating their evening meal. Maria was sitting in front of the house digging in the earth with a calf's jawbone that Önde had carved into shape for her.

"It sounds almost as if he's worried about something," said Önde.

"If only we had something to give him," said Ädla.

"I'm very sorry," said Önde, "that I didn't look after Blasius myself. He's the cleverest pig God's ever made."

193

"But I haven't cooked anything today," said Ädla, "and there's nothing left over."

"I would have taught him to draw the plough," said Önde. "And to get used to a bridle and a man on his back."

As Blasius swerved between the houses his rump hit against the walls so that splinters flew off the logs and the noise echoed through the empty houses.

Then he caught sight of Maria a long way ahead as she sat digging with the calf's jawbone. All his melancholy immediately fell from him as if someone had poured cold water over him. She was wearing a red frock that shone and shimmered in the evening sun. And he was upon her so fast that he didn't even understand himself how it happened. He lifted her on his snout and threw her up in the air, and she cried out in terror and delight – this was just how Önde used to surprise her and throw her up and catch her.

Ädla and Önde came rushing out, Önde still with a rabbit backbone in his teeth, but it was already too late. They stopped and stood there with their arms hanging at their sides and eyes wide with horror. The piece of rabbit fell from Önde's mouth. They were incapable of taking a single step or moving a single limb. Blasius was also standing absolutely still and looking at them. He knew them well, of course: they used to boil up fish with cabbage, it was Ädla and Önde.

But then Ädla began to tremble and whimper. There was a small piece of Maria still lying beside Blasius. Önde finally came to himself again, took Ädla in his arms and carried her in and put her to bed. Then he ran to fetch Borne and Könik.

Blasius had gone and lain down now beneath Avar's big rowan tree. He had rubbed his head a few times against the trunk, which was cool and rough, and immediately fallen asleep.

Borne fetched a long, sturdy rope and they helped one another to tie Blasius up. They made loops and tied his legs together and put a separate loop around his snout. He lay perfectly still and seemed not to mind what they did; perhaps he even raised his back leg a little so that they could get to it more easily. And they tethered him to the rowan tree, they gave the rope several turns round the trunk and tied triple knots.

Then Könik went to Nikolavus – it was at this point that he came and woke him up.

"Nikolavus," he said. "Nikolavus."

Nikolavus awoke with a start. He had slept so deeply this time that he hadn't even dreamed. He reached for the cover that Eira had laid out when she made the bed, and pulled it over himself.

And Könik held out something he had in his hand and asked: "Shall we bury what little there is left of Avar's Maria?"

But Nikolavus didn't understand.

So Könik had to explain. Once more he stammered and sobbed out an unbearably long and muddled and incredible story that he demanded Nikolavus should listen to and comprehend.

Yes, not just listen to it, but also take part in it and make it his own and complete it.

And Nikolavus looked at Könik and at the formless and unspeakable thing he was holding in his hand.

Then a shudder of terrible pain shot through him. It was as if someone were cutting into his chest with a knife, and there was a burning sensation inside his head as if someone were holding a flaming tar-stick against his eyes. He realized that he had made a fundamental error in thinking that what had been going on in Kadis was nothing but an entertaining and jocular story.

But he remained silent. Könik had to repeat his question. And he added a new one: "And what shall we do about Blasius now?"

At last Nikolavus sat up abruptly, as if a raging cramp had taken hold of him and jerked him upright, and he screamed at Könik in agonized incoherence. They should fetter the wild beast and lock him up so that other innocent and defenceless people didn't get gobbled up – but now they must leave him in peace in this hell-hole. As for Könik, he ought to be able to think of something himself. And as far as he, Nikolavus, was concerned, they could bury whatever bits of body they had wherever they wanted. And finally he bellowed at Könik to disappear from his sight.

Könik took the little remains of Maria to Önde. What Önde did with them no one knows. When Borne and Önde and Könik went to fetch Blasius later, he got up to come to meet them, and Avar's old rowan tree, which was firmly tied to him, was pulled up from the ground, roots and all. It was hard work untying the knots and disentangling Blasius from the tree, which had fallen on top of him. None of them mentioned the fact that they could have slaughtered him then and there. No, he was altogether too remarkable and his misdeed altogether too dreadful. Könik removed his bell, and Blasius let him do it. They set off with him, putting a rope round his front legs and dragging him the way you drag a heavy boat past rapids. He was as quiet and obedient as if he had indeed been slaughtered, and they managed to get him into the lock-up. They had to lift off the door and the door-posts. Önde pushed across a dried-up and mouldy piece of bread for him to eat. It had been lying in there since Könik's time inside.

And by the time everything had been done it was already morning. The sun was rising over the lower lake and the cows were calling for the women to milk them and it was time for the morning meal. Önde found a leather pouch under the roots of the rowan tree with ten little gold coins inside. There wasn't much left of the pouch, but the coins he took charge of himself.

Not much was achieved that day. The only one who did a day's work was Borne. What had happened to Blasius and Maria gave him the work he needed. He constructed the scaffold, and Könik helped him for a while with squaring the timbers and cutting the joints.

Two of them lay flat on their backs from morning to late evening: Ädla and Nikolavus. They lay staring out into empty nothingness.

Ädla couldn't cry, but Önde sat with her for long periods and cried in her stead. Yes, he took care of all her tasks, the milking and boiling the porridge and making the soup for the baby calf. But he said nothing. In a way, Maria had been his own child. How could he have found suitable words to say to Ädla when he could find none for himself?

Bera came over with two cheeses.

But Eira couldn't bring herself to visit Ädla.

She had a son herself who was temporarily away, of course. He would be coming back.

And she really had been on the way out to Blasius with his evening food, but just hadn't got there in time.

She brought in a dish of rabbit meat and nettle leaves for Nikolavus, but he didn't touch it.

His thoughts were confused and muddled, jumping all over the place. But by the afternoon they were beginning to come together.

The hag had certainly ridden him.

Her correct name was Succubus; she was known throughout

the educated world. She took countless forms but was nevertheless always the same.

It was Könik's hag who had been sent last night to suck the marrow and sap out of him. Könik had got rid of his own hag by setting it on him.

That Könik with the cloven face. The one who wanted to start legal proceedings against everyone and everything.

The accuser.

The accuser's correct name was Satan, the angel with the divided face, the one who plays tricks on God.

Yes, Könik who kept the devil as a domestic pig. This pig who could only be thought up and made flesh in a place at the end of the world to which God had not penetrated. Here in Kadis.

Yes, Kadis.

Not really a place at all, neither a town nor a village – no, an illusion and a figment of the imagination. A fiction where no one took responsibility for the people and what happened to them. A story without direction or aim, a frivolous game with human lives and holy matters. And cattle and rabbits.

No, he would indeed have to take Kadis in his charge. Everything could still be turned to his own advantage. Right down at the bottom of the fiction there were precious coins and pieces of silver lying buried. From now on he would decide and arrange everything. Strict and unbending and to the very letter.

Finally he got up and dressed and combed his hair that the hag had tangled, and shaved his cheeks with his knife. And he ate the food. Then he went to Önde and called to him to come out. Önde had put the rowan tree back up – he'd used stakes and put the roots back into the ground – and it would soon be in bloom again. He'd done it for Ådla's sake: it was Avar's rowan tree, after all.

First they said a few words about the grief that had afflicted the house. Önde had forgotten that the word existed – he repeated it several times, he even felt compelled to give himself the task of bearing it in to Ädla so that she could hear it too. Grief.

Then they talked for a long time about everything that was not generally known and that a passing visitor or a King's inspector might need to know about Kadis. Everything that had happened and everything that might happen. They sat down on the ground beneath the rowan tree, and Önde fetched them beer to drink. They talked about people and animals and houses and all the deeds and events and abominations that belonged to the past. Nikolavus informed himself properly. He should have gone to Önde immediately he arrived. It was to Önde that everyone should go when they arrived as strangers in Kadis. Then everything would have been all right from the beginning.


Könik saw him going to Önde. He went out and stood in front of the house and watched him. Borne could still be heard hammering and banging at the scaffold he was constructing. Borne wasn't very handy with things like that.

Then a man appeared walking towards him, someone who had walked past Bera's house, a stranger. He was walking fast, not bothering to look at the houses or the woodpiles or the frames where they used to dry their nets. When he reached Könik he asked whether this was Kadis.

Yes. This was Kadis.

"Then everything is in order," said the stranger.

He took off his rucksack and set it down at his feet. It was a sorry-looking little leather bag.

"It was a long way," he said, "from Umeå to Kadis."

He was a short, bald-headed man, with one shoulder much higher than the other and ears abnormally large. His beard was trimmed level with his shirt collar. He had a band with gold tassels on it round his forehead, and there were gold threads glittering in the cloth of his trousers.

"There's a man here called Önde," said Könik. "It's really him you should go to."

"I'm thirsty," said the stranger.

Könik went in and got a ladle-full of water from the water butt.

As he drank he fixed his gaze on the side of Könik's head that had the ear missing. Könik raised his hand and covered the spot. "It's not my fault, the ear," said Könik. "It was a knife that ran wild that did it."

"You could let your hair hang down over your ear," the stranger suggested.

"I never thought of that," said Könik.

When he had finished drinking he said who he was. His name was Magnus.

"We had a man called Magnus, too," said Könik. "He used to count the time for us. He cut notches in wooden staffs and he was the only one who understood the marks. So when he died, Önde burned the staffs."

Then this Magnus asked whether many had died in Kadis. And Könik erred rather on the excessive side when he answered.

"Everyone," he said.

"The priest was one of the first to die," he added. "After that no one even knew when the day of rest was."

"The Bishop has sent a whole lot of priests up to the north," said Magnus. "You'll soon have a new priest in Kadis."

"He was called Blasius," said Könik. "He was talking about it at the very moment he died."

"No order is possible without priests," said Magnus. "Without priests we buzz about like flies, without aims or rules. Confused and lost."

"Yet in a way," said Könik, without further explanation, "it was probably best for him that he died."

Nothing more was said about the priest. Instead Magnus asked: "The white fur on your shoes, what is it?"

"It's rabbit fur," said Könik. "We've had absurdly large numbers of rabbits here in Kadis."

And this word, rabbits, suddenly seemed uncannily fertile in Könik's mind. That one word begot and gave birth to a presentation so long and so detailed that he and the stranger, Magnus, were obliged to sit down to rest their legs. They sat on the bench where Könik usually killed the rabbits. He spoke about everything that a while ago he had told Nils, who was also called Nikolavus, everything that had happened since the Sickness came to Kadis. The left-hand half of his face was quivering with excitement, the right-hand side was slack with dejection and bitterness, his voice was trembling. He left no injustice and no lapse forgotten, he gave a detailed account of all the bewilderment and disorder – yes, everything that has been mentioned here he talked of once or even twice or more again. But he didn't say that there was a man with them now who had promised to re-establish law and order and to re-create Kadis.

Because he had gone to Önde, and hadn't come back yet.

When he finally finished, they both sat in silent thought for a while. The mosquitoes hummed around them. Then the man said: "I'm travelling on the King's business: I could easily set this little place on its feet again."

"Kadis was big," said Könik. "And we had a wall all round it."

"All that's needed," said Magnus, "is that the necessary truths are sought out. That order is restored. And that immutable laws are established. And of course there'll be a priest coming again soon."

And he outlined to Könik the procedure that seemed the most suitable to him. A day of judgement, quite simply.

"Though," he added, "I know nothing about the right way of making a net."

"So you would be able to sit in judgement over us," said Könik.

"Indeed."

"In the name of the King."

"If I didn't do it in the name of the King, it would be ineffective."

And how, Könik wanted to know, could he be so sure about his ability to carry it out?

But that was a question that was almost a joke. Magnus stroked his palm over his bald head and gave a short, sharp laugh. The King's men were all familiar with the law. It was knowledge of the law that had enabled him to become a King's man. In the service of the Crown he had to know all regulations and guidelines and customs, both those that were in use and all conceivable ones, and all measures and proclamations, whether already sealed or not yet devised.

"And where," said Könik, "did you get all this knowledge?"

"In the service of innumerable princes and lords," said Magnus. "And at seats of learning in foreign cities with the strangest names."

Könik sat rubbing the furrow in his brow. He was pondering.

"If a pig that was as big as a horse were brought before you," he said after a moment, "and the pig had swallowed a child that had been begotten by its own grandfather, how would you judge then?"

"Such disorder and confusion can't be possible," said Magnus.

"It could be imagined," said Könik.

"I would condemn him to lose his life," said Magnus unhesitatingly. "He should be broken on the wheel and his snout should be set up on a stake. But nothing need be done about the child – the pig would have already administered justice.

"The size of the pig," he went on, "would not be relevant to the case."

And then he said: "But the pig you're imagining would also have to have a master. An owner and farmer."

"Yes," said Könik.

"He would unquestionably have to be hanged along with the pig."

And then Könik asked whether he had actually been sent by the King for the very purpose of restoring laws and customs, whether that was the business on which he had come. Whether that was really what he was, a restorer of order and harmony for the King.

At that, Magnus gave a start and straightened his back as if the word "business" had struck him a blow. He had let himself become so engrossed in Könik's story of the hardship and distress in Kadis that he had totally forgotten his real task, and he turned to Könik now with an ugly expression on his face.

"I'm looking for a man," he said. "I've followed him all the way from southern Sweden and now to here."

"Some kind of criminal?" Könik asked.

"A King's man," said Magnus. "Or to put it more correctly: a man who did serve the King, one of the most trusted men." But during the time of the Sickness, when lawlessness and confusion took over the world, evil had permeated and distorted his mind and his thoughts. His body had continued to flourish but the Sickness had deformed his soul. And he used a word from foreign lands: chaos.

"It's incomprehensible," said Könik, "that such things can happen. That a person's mind can be infected like that."

Well, this false King's man was travelling through the country now and stealing and cheating. He was an unrestrained embezzler and a shameless robber, the man was a complete fiction and a fabrication through and through. He stole silver from merchants and rings from bishops; from wives their modesty and from peasants their daily bread. And now he, Magnus, had been entrusted with the task of hunting and catching this rogue and trickster, to track him down and, with the help of honest subjects, to seize him, dead or alive.

"Well," said Könik, "we all have our tasks and missions. We are all tested to the utmost."

The King for his part demanded nothing less than this rogue's head, impaled on a stake or delivered in a leather bag. He would be content with nothing else.

And what did it look like, then, this head?

Well, he himself would say that the man looked exactly like a criminal. But he'd often heard others say that he was quite good-looking. He shaved his beard every day and his hair looked like combed flax and he had a silver-threaded band round his forehead. When he said that it was a good-looking, perhaps even handsome head, his face contorted in distaste.

"And he must have had a name, too?" said Könik. "This criminal King's man."

"Nils – yes, Nils. But as the King's man he bore the name of Nikolavus."

"A fine name," said Könik. "Almost a ceremonial one."

What had happened, then, was that his tracks, which of course weren't tracks in the usual sense, but vague evidence and hearsay and reports of dishonest and unscrupulous actions, had now led Magnus here to Kadis.

"But I'll soon find him now," he said. "Because this is where the world ends."

"Yes," said Könik. "More or less."

Eira came out to them at that moment. And Könik asked her whether she thought she could find any food for this man who had come from a long way away and was a stranger here, something he could either eat straight away if need be or keep till he could stave off his hunger no longer.

So the question was whether a man like this, a stranger, had been seen in Kadis, a villain with a head like the one described.

"We get so many strangers here," said Könik. "Some days we do nothing else but give them food and show them the way."

"What way?" said Magnus abruptly and suspiciously. "The path stops here."

"Well," said Könik vaguely, "perhaps not paths exactly, but there are directions and bearings that we can point out."

Magnus now repeated his question about the man he was seeking and described him in a little more detail, the way he sounded when he spoke and how he moved and the silver chains round his wrists.

"You must give me time to think about it," said Könik. "I'll have to search my memory. Let's talk for a bit, then I can make up my mind whether I've seen him or not."

"Well," said Magnus, "I'm not in any particular hurry. And this is where the world ends anyway. He can't escape me much longer."

Indeed, he even said: "When I find him and have to kill him it's going to hurt me. All life is so painfully dear to me."

And as he said this, his face again contorted in distaste.

"There are people here who can help you," said Könik. "One's called Borne, he's the hangman. Another man's called Önde."

"You mentioned Önde," said Magnus. "You said I ought to go to him."

"He's never at a loss," said Könik. "He's a harmless creature. But never at a loss when it comes to giving advice."

"I could," said Magnus, "allow myself a day or two's rest. I could offer you the help you need with the most necessary and self-evident things, with law and order. In the name of the King."

"You know," said Könik, "that you've come such an awfully long way that you've got yourself caught up in a complicated story."

"Of course," said Magnus. "A King's man must keep himself informed about everything."

When he clapped himself on his bald head his palm came away red with blood from all the mosquitoes.

"Yes," said Könik. "This matter of law and order. What the nature of the law really is. In its innermost essence."

205

"If everyone were law-abiding," said Magnus, "there'd be no need for the law. But the defenceless need protection, the peaceable must have their peace, and the foolish and the wrongheaded must be told the truth. And the violent must be punished."

"It's as simple as that," said Könik.

"Yes, it's as simple as that. Justice is like an invisible creature that flees before us. As long as we keep chasing it, we have it. It's the constant seeking for law and justice that constitutes law and justice."

"We had it here in Kadis," said Könik. "But the Sickness carried it off."

"Law and justice cannot die," said Magnus. "There will always come a time of restoration and rehabilitation and repair. All confusion and disorder and disintegration is just semblance and illusion. Law and order endures in secret. Truth and justice are not a conjuring trick. And the law is not just a story with an arbitrary ending."

"The law," said Könik.

"The law," said Magnus, "is what is natural and self-evident. The law may be written or unwritten. But it can never be cast in doubt or eradicated."

Eira came out then with the food, which she had wrapped in a piece of cloth. It was of course dried rabbit. Magnus thanked her and sat there for a while holding it in his hand. He was wondering whether he should eat it or not, but then he pushed it down into his rucksack.

"So the law," said Könik, "is always exactly the same."

"Yes," said Magnus, "it is eternally the same. Whole and indivisible."

"You're completely sure about that?" said Könik.

"Yes, there can never be any doubt about it. One law. One justice. One judge.

"Two systems of law and order," he stated, "are synonymous with confusion."

Könik really wanted to be certain about that, he enlisted other words to help, and images too. Justice and truth, then, could not be like a face that is cleft in two, with one half elusively indecisive and the other half frighteningly determined and undaunted, or like a rabbit that is incessantly conceiving and giving birth and running around all over the place in derisive and godless caprice. Or like two male figures, one tall and fair and smiling and the other dark and gloomy.

"No," said Magnus, the King's man. "The law is immutable and incontestable, it is the most unified of all the unities of Creation and it can only appear in one single form. It is a state of peace and reconciliation. A single source of light."

"So if you've chosen a restorer of order and a judge, you should stick to him, then," said Könik.

"Yes, you should concentrate on eradicating all other judges and restorers of order."

And Magnus added: "It is in times of trouble that justice is in demand and manifests itself. How childlike man is in his joy and how understanding in his grief."

Könik pondered for some time.

Finally he said:

"Now I know."

"What is it you know?" asked Magnus, the man of the Crown.

And Könik said that now he could remember that stranger with the silver-threaded band round his forehead, the one who was a trickster and deceiver and in essence nothing but a fiction and a fabrication, he remembered him coming to Kadis. Yes, he really did.

"And what happened?"

"We gave him food. And pointed out which direction he should take."

"So he was going on further?"

"Yes. He was going on."

"But where to? Everything ends here. There are no other villages beyond Kadis."

"Yes, there are," said Könik. "It's not widely known, but there's a place called Maidige. It's over the other side of the river, further inland."

"And that's where he was going?"

"Yes. That's where he was going."

Magnus gave a deep sigh and straightened his back once more and turned his face to Könik. It was haggard and grim and determined. It was one of the ugliest faces Könik had ever seen.

"Then I've got no choice," he said.

"No," said Könik. "And if people have a choice they have to choose one thing or the other. So they still end up without any choice."

Then Magnus asked: "Could you point out the right direction for me too?"

"Yes," said Könik. "I can do that."

So they got up and walked past the houses and past the wall that was now just rotted stakes and down the hill towards the river. They followed the bank upstream, walking slowly because Magnus had already come a long way and was far from rested. He had a tendency to waddle and a strange way of jerking his legs with every step, as if his decisiveness and resolve were in his hips and knee joints. They didn't speak. Könik was just going with him part of the way to point out the right direction.

Except that Könik turned to him briefly and said: "In a way we could well have needed you in Kadis too."

When they had passed two sharp bends and the biggest curve in the river, Könik stopped. It was almost like a lake, the river was wide and there were stones sticking up here and there in the water.

And it was now that he pointed.

"You just cross straight over here," he said. "Everyone who wants to get to Maidige goes this way. And then you continue on up the other bank."

"A strange name," said Magnus. "Maidige."

"It's probably Lappish," said Könik. "As far as I know it

doesn't mean anything. And you can walk for as long as you like. We have light here all the time."

So this man Magnus stepped out into the water. He didn't look as if he felt the cold. And when he got part of the way out he turned round and raised his hand in thanks to Könik for having helped him by pointing out the right direction. He would eat the dried rabbit on the other side. When the water reached his waist he began to climb up on the stones and jump between them. He seemed to be surprisingly light and sure of foot. Finally he took a dreadfully long leap which even so turned out to be too short, and the whirlpools and the current carried him off. The river took him. No living creature had ever managed to cross there.


Just as Könik and Magnus were making their way down to the river bank, the conversation between Önde and Nikolavus was coming to an end. This is how it concluded:

"The pig, then."

"Yes. We'll have to try to handle him somehow."

"And Könik."

"Yes. I hadn't thought about that. But it will probably do him good."

And Eira didn't mention the other stranger to Nikolavus when he came back. After all, he'd already gone again, and you probably shouldn't bother a King's man unnecessarily with chat and gossip. Soon Könik arrived too and they ate their evening porridge.

Before Nikolavus went to bed he hung up his robe with the white cross on it on the wall above the bed. He turned it so that the cross was on the outside. The cross is the surest defence against the hag.

So Blasius was dragged through Kadis once more. They lifted out the door-posts and the door of the lock-up and tied the rope round him and heaved and hauled him to the chapel. He had been imprisoned for a whole day and a whole night, and he hadn't much will to live left in him. His hide was torn to shreds on the stones and gravel. But he was completely silent and just let his head and legs hang loose and dangle and jerk to and fro on the bumpy ground. He was magnificent in his suffering. And they tethered him in the chapel.

Never before in Kadis had an animal been tried and judged. Perhaps in previous times when everything was natural and self-evident and in proper order no animals had ever committed any crimes.

Now, when they had all taken their places, they avoided looking at Blasius. He stank horribly and his crime was dreadful and they had all been so deeply attached to him.

Yes, all the people of Kadis were there. The women were standing by the door, the men sitting on the squared logs. Even Ädla was there. She had a black veil over her head that she'd made from one of Avar's old shirts, as if she had only now become a widow. Könik was looking at Nikolavus. During the night Könik's face had split so irretrievably that he was having to hold one eyelid up with his forefinger, on the side that had completely collapsed in terror; and his other eye was not even blinking – that half of his face was as hard and rigid as if he himself had carved it from an alder root.

Nikolavus declared that he wanted to restore law and order here in Kadis quickly and would show no leniency. He himself

– even in his own body – had experienced the terror of how bad things were. There was no time now for deliberation and full and formal enquiry and administration of justice according to the rules – no, everything must be decided straight to the point and without lengthy consideration. There would be judgements here, and nothing more.

Könik's gaze was upon him. Nikolavus was after all one single person, he was immutable and incontestable, he sat whole and undivided on the priest's chair, and now he had no clinking silver chains and he had only two rings on his fingers. One of them could well be the King's.

He would like to deal quickly with the simplest petty matters. One of those here had become perhaps rather too fond of a heifer. But there was no likelihood of ascertaining the facts and the heifer was dead. Someone who was also dead had begotten a child who also happened to be his grandchild and who now was dead. Mere trifles. And one of them had enticed a trader to stay in Kadis and die there and had kept the silver in his leather bag for himself.

"I tried to comfort him in his last moments," said Önde. "I gave him beavers' musk glands."

"But the silver," said Nikolavus. "The silver."

"I've only been minding it," said Önde. "On behalf of the rightful owner."

"Who then can the rightful owner be?" Nikolavus asked.

"Yes," said Önde, "I've thought about that a lot."

"Then I will tell you," said Nikolavus. "The silver belongs to the King. If there are no other heirs, then the King is always the rightful heir."

Könik looked at Önde. So they were at least achieving some sort of justice here.

"Yes," said Önde. "That's natural and self-evident. Now that you say it."

"It must be handed over to the Court," said Nikolavus.

And Önde's face trembled suddenly as if it also was about to crack and divide in two. He had thought that he had come to an agreement with Nikolavus, they had talked to one another for a whole afternoon under the rowan tree. The only thing he could think of to say was a few words about Olavus the trader: "But his death was a happy release."

So far, so good. And now to further matters. Ownership marks had been carved everywhere on objects and on walls. Some people had taken offence at the form and possible meaning of the marks, two deep notches with a shallower cut across them, so beautifully done that one could imagine the knife had flown forward and carved them of its own volition, by its own power.

When he mentioned the knife, Könik's hand went up involuntarily to the ear that was missing.

But these marks were something that time would heal, time and sun and decay, they were alas so transient, and he would not pass judgement on the knife nor on the hand that may have held it.

Also, someone had appropriated various things that the dead, in all the haste, had taken with them to their graves. That was only human, or at least forgivable, perhaps even understandable. The only question was: Who was actually the rightful owner of these small objects that had been dug up from the earth?

And he fell silent. They were all silent.

Finally Önde sighed: "The King."

Yes, indeed. It was as simple as that. Deliver them up to the Court, then everything would be settled.

First he was called Nils, then Nikolavus, and now he was simply called "the Court". He spoke fast, so fast that the words sometimes came out of his mouth all joined together or truncated, and he was not lisping. He wanted this story to move quickly and unfalteringly now and come soon to its rightful conclusion.

On the subject of the actual digging up or burying or whereabouts of this or that, and of the dead who in fact were rotting so fast that they could safely be left out of consideration – they were absorbed by the earth like flowing water – he had only one thing to say and he wanted to repeat it again forcefully now: Mere trifles.

It was then that Könik learned the word. It was a strict, judgemental phrase but at the same time a liberating one: Mere trifles.

And Nikolavus continued to recount everything that he knew had happened in Kadis, large as well as small. It was Önde's account, but part of it was probably also Könik's, and it was being examined and broken down and judged. The whole thing was very familiar to Könik and yet so peculiarly alien. It was this that had tormented him and been the hag of his nightmare. Occasionally the judge laughed, a short, sharp, high-pitched laugh, he rubbed his chin with the palm of his left hand and clicked his fingers and his two rings sparkled. Mere trifles, he proclaimed. Mere trifles, all the rest, to be passed over in silence.

And everything without an owner or an inheritor reverted to the King.

Of course they all knew – yes, even Bera understood it and Borne had a vague suspicion of it – that the whole thing was a joke and a conjuring trick, but it was so formal and serious and magnificent that they all went along with it in meek obedience. They were not in a position to dismiss or remain outside the course of events just because it was a trick and an illusion. And they weren't entirely certain, they hadn't been certain of anything for a long time. A certainty such as Eira's that Kare would come back, that was an irrational exception.

Even that was now briefly mentioned, that a baby had been stolen, a son.

Könik stood up at that point and said: "That was my fault, it was me who brought the idea to Kadis that little children could be stolen."

There was silence. No one even said "mere trifles". There was a tiny weak whimper from Eira, but she said nothing. And the strange thing was that Nikolavus didn't feel the need to say anything for a long time.

Then Könik sat down. And he added: "But I think it was Önde who did it."

Once again there was a deep silence. But at last Önde said: "I can't for the life of me remember doing it."

"I saw the tracks," said Könik. "And I know you."

"If I was the one who did it," said Önde, "then I must have been in a sort of trance. If I did it, it must have been because I didn't know what I was doing."

Eira drew in her breath and took a short step forward as if she intended to run up to the men and start screaming at them and scratching them with her nails and hitting them, no matter which of them, but she stopped herself straight away – yes, in mid-step – she calmed down again suddenly and felt more confident than before. If it was only Önde who had taken Kare, then it was even more certain that he would come back again.

"In a trance," said Könik, "you'd be as stiff as a rod and just go slowly straight ahead, feeling your way with your hands."

"No, may the devil take me," said Önde. "In a trance you might do anything at all. Beget children and slaughter animals and attack people with knives and ride strangers in the shape of a hag. When people are in a trance, they're like starved pigs left without food or attention."

"And that's exactly how you were," said Könik.

"I don't know anything," said Önde. "I just wanted to help you to think about how things could have happened with Kare."

"Are you perhaps in a trance even now?" said Könik derisively.

"No," said Önde with care. "If you're in a trance, you certainly know you are."

"People should always know what they're doing," said Könik. "You can't go round like a sleepwalker." And now he raised his voice so that he was almost screaming at Önde. "If you make yourself blind and deaf, you'll fall into every pit – yes, into any and every abyss."

But Önde was calm and humble. "I can't for the life of me remember anything," he said. "But if it does turn out that I stole him, then I suppose it's possible that I did know what I was doing."

"Now," said Könik, "now the truth is creeping out."

Önde was silent for a long time. He was plucking at his beard with his thumb and finger and his eyes were roving around the walls. It was as if he was unsure whether he should say anything at all now that he was being accused of telling the truth. He turned to see whether Eira was still there, and he looked across at Nikolavus as if expecting some sort of help from him.

But Nikolavus was cleaning his nails.

Eira had been wearing on her head the piece of cloth that Önde had pressed upon her. Now she had taken it off and put it under her feet to stand on.

The silver chain that he had given her and that she usually wore round her neck was in her hand. She would be glad to be able to give that to the Court and be free of it.

Finally Önde said: "It might have been that I wanted to save him from death."

"Death?" said Könik.

"Once when you had it in your mind to kill him."

"Me?" said Könik. "Kill Kare?"

"I came in once," said Önde, "and you had your hands round his neck."

And Könik said: "I can't for the life of me remember doing that."

"I came at the last minute," said Önde. "You were just about to squeeze your fingers tight. We had to put you in the lock-up."

"If I did that," said Könik, "it must have been because I didn't know what I was doing. I must have been in a sort of trance."

And he turned to see whether Eira was still there and he

215

scratched his beard and he pressed his finger on the eyelid that was falling down the whole time.

"I don't understand anything," he said. "If what you're saying is the truth."

"Have I ever," Önde asked, "said anything other than the truth?"

"Then I must have been wanting to guard him and protect him. I wanted to hold my hands over him to stop anyone taking him."

"People should always know exactly what they are doing in every detail," said Önde.

"I wanted to hold him tight for ever," said Könik. "I wanted to make sure that nothing could happen to him. With Kadis the way it was."

And so they went on, one accusing the other, the other defending himself with accusations, and every accusation was stronger and more merciless than the last. They were completely pitiless and yet completely helpless – they came off quite badly against each other. They dug up everything that had happened in the past. Önde now recalled the time when Könik had chased him with the knife to kill him, and Könik remembered the knife that Önde had used on his ear. Könik wasn't trying any longer to hold his face together, he mostly sat covering it with both hands.

Blasius stood where he was. He was tethered so that he couldn't lie down. The women stood where they had been put, by the door; the cows were in the forest, Bera had Jasper with her in his basket, and the small animals had been fed for the whole day. And Nikolavus sat smiling absent-mindedly and cleaning his fingernails. A King's man had to have nails whiter than snow. The story was running away with itself, he didn't need to do anything, it was hopping about in twists and turns like a frightened, hunted rabbit. He could simply wait for the right moment.

Könik and Önde became more and more unreasonable and

shameless towards one another. One was accused of letting the wall collapse and destroying the nets beyond repair, and the other of mixing up the names of the days so that they might now be called anything at all, and of having burned the staffs on which Magnus had notched up the passage of time and kept count of it, and of having lied and pretended about the years and the seasons and the weeks so that time had become one gigantic muddle that could no longer be unravelled. And both of them had encouraged the rabbits and fed them and helped them to multiply so that they now consumed every bit of greenery in Kadis and would soon be swallowing up the houses and chattels.

But Borne sat there in complete silence. Except for one single occasion when he opened his mouth.

"Önde promised me a piece of silver," he said, "if I could tell him the difference between seriousness and a joke. I've puzzled a lot about that silver."

At that Nikolavus looked quickly up from his nails and said: "Whose can that silver be?"

"Yes," said Borne, "it must presumably be the King's."

Deeper and deeper into the long-forgotten past Könik and Önde questioned each other. They were amazed themselves that they had such an infinite amount to accuse each other of – yes, and also that it was each other and not any of the other people, living and dead, that they held responsible. They dredged up all manner of things and events that don't belong here, lies and deceits and quarrels from their early childhood – and they even heaped on each other the misdeeds of their forefathers. They carried on for the whole morning without faltering or tiring. But in the end they were no longer aware of what they were saying. Neither of them noticed when Ädla got fed up with the whole thing and left. They yelled their charges and justifications and insults and oaths as if in a trance.

It is impossible to say how long this went on.

But finally Nikolavus thought that the right moment had come. He had nothing to gain from the two of them killing each

217

other. The sun had long since passed its midday height; in the distance the cows were mooing as they wended their way home from the forest. He inspected his nails once more, then looked up and stopped them with a single conclusive phrase.

"Mere trifles," he cried. "Mere trifles."

Önde and Könik broke off in the midst of their ranting and raging and fell silent.

Yes, of course he understood their situation, and it was completely unnecessary for them to fight and wrangle any more and threaten to annihilate each other. For him it had been enough to take one single look at this place for the distress and wretchedness to be obvious, to see what a curse had befallen those who lived here, what a storm of God's wrath had passed through Kadis and how the whole place and people and even part of the surrounding area had been devastated and almost wiped out. He realized that the calamity had come upon them like a heath fire, they had been taken by surprise. How childlike man is in his joy, he said, and how he loses all reason in his grief.

But he wanted to reassure them that what had happened to Kadis had happened more or less throughout the whole world. He knew that well, since he had journeyed extensively over the world, but for those who lived imprisoned in this preposterous story it wasn't easy to know what plagues and pestilence had attacked the far ends of the country or even the regions nearby. No, their ignorance was necessary and intended by their Maker, it was a result of the whole design, not to say order, that controlled their lives. They ought to know, however, that there were towns which had been laid waste, villages where people had eaten one another, places that no longer had so much as a name.

If truth be told, they should count themselves lucky that their home was Kadis.

In particular they should count themselves lucky for one special and miraculous reason: they had a guilty party. More precisely, two guilty parties.

If God really wants to punish a place in the extreme, he said, He fills it with the innocent.

Here, then, they had Blasius, this astonishing and hideous pig. It was he who should be tried and judged. Many had gone astray and sinned in Kadis, but it was he who had perpetrated the crime which surpassed all other small lapses and misdeeds, where the phrase "mere trifle" was no longer appropriate. As for trial – well, his guilt was so obvious that a trial in the normal sense of the word was hardly necessary.

Then he went on to describe exhaustively and extensively the crime that Blasius had committed, including a lengthy exposition on Blasius as a rarity and a lower form of life.

And now Eira called out: "He's really Önde's. It was Önde who delivered the sow and brought him to us."

But nobody seemed to hear her.

Önde sat at the front and combed his beard with the comb he'd acquired a fearfully long time ago, long before the beginning of this story, in exchange for his wife Cecilia.

It had to be said, of course, that Blasius was a dumb animal, said Nikolavus, and that animals are born and live and die as if in one long-drawn-out sleep, that he thus hadn't known what he was doing, that he had acted as if in a trance. But he had known that he was hungry, he had known how to break out of his sty, he had known how to find his way to the defenceless little girl. It would be utterly vain and absurd to try to establish a border or dividing line between thought and thoughtlessness, between knowing and not knowing, between consciousness and trance. All deeds were fundamentally constituted in the same way: they were carried out, and more than that one could never know – the idea and the intention and the will were embodied in the actual carrying out of the deed. By their deeds shall all living creatures be judged. Over all our deeds there hangs a veil of trance.

Blasius had pricked up his ears. He grunted occasionally, but only rather weakly and feebly. The light from the apertures in the walls shone on him. He looked even more enormous here than he had in the sty. He had grown up in the sty and everyone had got used to comparing his size with that of the sty. Now when they saw him against the timber pillars that supported the roof and against the logs of the walls his size was all the more unbelievable. His body was so solid and massive and bulky that they would have liked to think that he was only a figment of their imagination.

But Eira thought she could see the fat already beginning to shrink. He had been starved for a whole day and a whole night, and she could see small fine wrinkles in his skin.

Nor, Nikolavus wished to point out, was Blasius simply a pig. No, he was also a sign and a symbol: he represented, in his unrestrained excess, their situation which was now about to be transformed into peace and clarity and lawfulness.

As they all knew, he, Nikolavus, was a widely-travelled envoy of the King. In foreign cities with the strangest names he had seen animals of all kinds brought up before their judges, he had seen goats and dogs taken to the gallows, and bulls and pigs and even rats bend their heads beneath the executioner's axe. What was to befall this pig was the same as was meted out to all those of his sort throughout the whole educated world.

Enough then about Blasius. There remained this man Könik.

He would be brief. The cows were already lowing for their milkers and a square meal wouldn't go amiss and this everlasting talking and lofty speechifying was tiring him. He had also talked vastly more and at greater length than is evident from the story. But nevertheless he could not content himself in Könik's case either with the words "mere trifles". No, Könik could not under any circumstances be considered guilty of mere trifles.

And so to Könik.

With all his talk of confusion and disorder and injustice he had himself caused confusion and disorder and injustice. By conveying the rumour about the snatching of children he had caused his own child to be snatched away. He had drawn a knife against his neighbour and caused his own ear to be cut off. He had also insulted and slandered his neighbour. He had fattened his pig into a beast of prey of such size that it could hardly even be squeezed into a story. He had watched over his wife so badly that she had set the wild animal loose. He had sent the hag that dwelt in his own breast to ride and beat black and blue a highly-respected stranger who was a guest in his house. That was a fact perhaps not known to the other members of the Court, but that is what had happened. He had enticed and induced a King's man to play the part of judge, a practical joke that had been pushed here to the utmost point, where the ambiguous is transformed into the unambiguous. In short: With his cleft face and the blackness in his soul he had caused public offence and disturbed peace and order and security in Kadis. Indeed, charge upon charge could be laid against him, all through the night's long light hours – yes, even unto eternity.

What could Könik do? He had taken out a piece of birch bark and was chewing it. He could have collapsed in a state of paralysis. He could have stood up and walked off, like a sleepwalker. He could have thrown himself upon Nikolavus and killed him and delivered his head to the King. But what sort of law and order and clarity would that have been, what standard or continuity would have been accomplished, what pattern or shape or model would thus have been manifested? No, this was doubtless the way it was meant to be, authority is always just as ridiculous as Nikolavus and yet just as compelling and inescapable. So Könik chewed on his birch bark – the chewing of his jaws held his face together. As he chewed, he said: "Yes, what you say may be true. Except the bit about the hag – I didn't even know that myself."

Then he added: "I've also got two gold coins that came from Olavus the trader. I buried them an awfully long time ago in the warm earth beneath Eira's left shoulder-blade."

They could proceed, then, to the verdict?

"Yes."

So Nikolavus pronounced judgement. He introduced it by saying that all life was so painfully dear to him. It was a long and complicated and barely comprehensible verdict, full of words from foreign cities with the strangest names. But the essential points were nevertheless understandable. He asked them whether they were all in agreement. They were silent for a moment; then Önde answered for the whole of Kadis. "Yes," he said. "Yes."


Nikolavus could have let it all end there, he could have said that he had tricked them for long enough and that this was the conclusion he had imagined. Yes, that when the cuts and bruises from the hag had been at their most painful, he had even imagined a much crueller and bloodier end in Könik's case; but that mercy must be shown. Without mercy all jokes and all tricks lose their effect.

In the evening all the King's property was brought to him. He poured it all into two leather bags that Ädla had inherited from Avar and that she gladly gave him. And Könik lent him a yoke.

He could have taken his leave of Kadis then and trudged off like a royal mule, weighed down by his dignity and the other burdens. But he stayed there overnight. No one should get the idea that he was fleeing. But he slept now in Avar's house, Ädla's house, against the same wall as Önde. And Önde did not get up and beat him to death, that would have been too impossible a crime against the established rules, not of justice and the lawful order, but of the story.

Könik slept in the lock-up with Blasius. Blasius let him use the thigh of his right foreleg as a pillow.

Now someone might have remembered something that had been said an awfully long time ago about a vanquished dragon and his wretched master. They hanged Blasius, all three of them had to help one another, Önde and Borne and Könik, he was to hang until he was dead. The scaffold creaked and bowed but they got him up nevertheless, he didn't kick out against them. His flesh was soft and quivering, as if he'd been left to simmer in water for several days. He hung with his black part downwards and light part upwards. And then it was Könik's turn. He was to hang just long enough for the hag to fall off him. The rope was tied two turns round his chest. On the King's orders, or as good as, he was to be drained of the hag and his senseless and uncontrolled behaviour in the way that a rabbit is drained of its blood. He was to be cut down before evening. Borne said this was deplorable, to hang a man and yet not hang him, but that for Könik's sake they should, he supposed, be grateful. Moderation in all things, he added. The stocks, where formerly they used to confine those who needed to come to their senses, had been rebuilt by Önde to fit Jalte's bull.

So Könik hung there and dangled so that he would become a little wiser and humbler, and no one wondered at it. It was an incredibly long time since anyone had been filled with wonder in Kadis. When the absurd became the normal they'd had to get used to being ashamed of feeling a sense of wonder. All their misery was no less wondrously natural and self-evident. God knows what might have happened long ago if they had had a sense of wonder. Those who don't have a feeling of wonder live for the most part in serenity and feel secure in their state of trance. The act of waking up, any kind of awakening, consists of a feeling of wonder and nothing else. Babies feel a sense of wonder when they are born and see their first daylight; and those who have lain paralyzed like a bird feigning death and are then cured feel a sense of wonder; and those who arise from the dead feel a sense of wonder. But this very morning Borne and Bera had been almost unmercifully tempted to feel wonder. Borne had felt inside her mouth with his tongue and found something sharp and smooth that had not been there before, and he had opened her jaws and held her towards the light, and there he had clearly seen that her first teeth were on their way up out of the flesh. But then they had restrained themselves and just said that, well, it was probably high time and that she might as well get her teeth now that Jasper was getting his. He had bitten blood from her nipples the night before. And her teeth wouldn't be any good yet awhile anyway for biting off the umbilical cords of newborn kids.

It can also happen that one single occasion of wonder can be a feeling so intense that it lasts a person for the rest of his life. He never again wants to raise his eyes even fleetingly. That was the case with Ädla, who on one occasion had been so filled with wonder that she thought she was going to die.

There she was, and she couldn't comprehend that anything remarkable or strange was happening – well, no, this was just another day in Kadis.

But Eira stood there weeping in amazement. It has been mentioned before that she was lamentably small – yes, that she was so short that if Könik had come upon the word "dwarf" he might in consternation have used it of her. Up to now her smallness had not been of any particular import, it might even have seemed irrelevant. But now it did indeed take on significance. She was inadequate. She herself thought that she was not only short, but that she was shrinking. She became so slight and shrivelled that she might disappear at any moment. She didn't come up as far as the knots that Borne had tied round

224

the poles, she couldn't give Blasius or Könik a cup of drink or a piece of bread – no, not even if she stood on tiptoe could she reach up a comforting hand to Blasius' hooves or the soles of Könik's feet. A person cannot feel weaker or smaller or more lamentable and still feel like a human being.

Nikolavus was standing ready for departure. He had the silver-threaded band around his forehead and his own bag on his back, and from the yoke he carried across his shoulders hung the leather bags with all the gold and silver that there had been in Kadis and that now belonged to the King. He had put two rabbitskins that he'd got from Önde beneath the yoke to prevent sores. He was not hurrying. He knew that a single incautious movement of his body might be enough for him no longer to be able to keep the reins on this fickle and fragile and rabbit-like fiction. The whole story could be in danger of turning into illusion and go rushing off completely out of control if he were to hurry in any way. But he would soon be trudging down towards the river; he would stride slowly and carefully as if he were walking in a trance.

Anything at all could have happened now. Eira might have fetched the little axe that Könik had made specially for her and set upon Borne. It might have occurred to Borne to cut short Blasius' suffering with the broad-bladed axe. Önde might have drawn his knife and killed Nikolavus. Indeed, any of them might have killed any of the others. But that was not how it was going to be, that was not the intention.

Eira's eyes were fixed first on Könik, then on Blasius. And when she looked carefully at Könik she could see that something was happening to his face.

At first he kept his eyes closed: it looked as if he was asleep. He was full of confusion and a nauseating and sweaty feeling of shame and emptiness. But in the end he opened his eyelids a little, it wouldn't make any difference. He could look at the rabbits, he could let his gaze leap about for a while with the rabbits.

But he soon had to open his eyes a little wider. He couldn't see any rabbits.

He turned his head this way and that and squinted and peered. But no rabbits.

Finally he opened his eyes wide. No, not a single rabbit to be seen. And he thought about it, tentatively and hesitantly. No, he hadn't seen a rabbit for several days. Now there were not even rabbits.

But since he had at last opened his eyes, he might as well look round at all there was to see; he wouldn't bother to close them.

He had not only been humiliatingly brought down, but also strung up, indeed even elevated, so that he saw everything from above.

He saw the grass. It was green.

He saw a bird, a yellowhammer. It was pulling a worm out of the ground.

And the houses. They were shimmering like pieces of silver. They were standing where they had always stood.

He could see the birch grove beyond the chapel. It was like one enormous nettle flower.

He saw the sunshine. It was strong and burning, but as refreshing as spring water.

And he was filled with wonder.

It was now that Eira saw something happening to his face. That furrow was getting shallower – yes, down over the nose it was completely gone.

Then Könik turned his head and looked at Blasius. He was no longer hanging limp and listless – no, he was struggling and fighting and flailing now with all his might. He was twisting his body and kicking his hooves and hitting out wildly on all sides with his head, trying to free himself. The scaffold swayed and the rope creaked and groaned. Borne's knots whined and squeaked. He was after all the mightiest pig in the kingdom. And even though he had the rope round his neck he bellowed just as Avar's bull had done that time the current carried him off.

Könik looked carefully at Blasius. Such an awful lot of life and flesh in a single body. Such boundless desperation and determination. Such a harrowing display of the greatness and wretchedness of existence, half white, half black. You could indeed feel a sense of wonder.

He had never really understood Blasius.

It was actually not just Blasius hanging there and battling for his life. Könik could see that Blasius encompassed something far greater. It was Kadis, not to say God's whole Creation, that was struggling and suffering there on the rope. Even his fat seemed to be taut with effort and terror and persistence.

And Könik felt the furrow in his brow finally disappearing. He looked at Eira and Ädla and the others standing there and he saw the houses and the footpaths running so orderly and sensibly between the houses. He had never experienced such powerful sunlight, and he became aware of how right and proper and natural and self-evident everything was – it was as if Kadis had suddenly been cured and healed before his very own wondering eyes.

And he summoned all his strength and gripped the rope, he tensed his flesh so that his whole body looked as if it were covered in bumps and swellings, and he kicked and twisted and flailed exactly like Blasius.

But when Nikolavus saw that, he began moving off carefully down towards the river bank.

The knots that Borne had tied tore apart as if they had been tied in play by a little child. And Könik shouted out the words of liberation, "Mere trifles!" so that it echoed over the whole of Kadis. He broke loose from the story in which he had been imprisoned and jumped down to the ground. He landed firmly but softly on both feet and set off in hot pursuit of Nikolavus. And it was as if Könik had given a secret sign to Borne and Önde, as if "mere trifles" had been the password they had been

227

waiting for. They too ran after Nikolavus, who had no chance whatsoever of escaping, since he had much too heavy a weight hanging across his shoulders.

Borne grabbed him round the arms and chest and Könik and Önde relieved him of his burdens. And for a moment they stood there with the leather bags, almost as if they were once again on the point of becoming irresolute and confused. But Könik soon achieved clarity and order again.

"Gold and silver," he said, "should be buried. And I know no one who can do it better than you, Önde."

That was how simple it was.

And while Borne stayed there and held Nikolavus, Könik and Önde ran back to the scaffold and cut Blasius down. He was slightly blue, but seemed nevertheless to be in amazingly good spirits. He had never really in his heart given up all hope. He shook himself a few times so that his flesh rippled and trembled like the surface of water whipped up by the wind. And Könik said:

"Can you imagine anything more stupid? Hanging a pig!"

Then Blasius rushed off as fast as his legs could carry him. There was a hollow rumbling in the empty houses as his flanks knocked against corners and walls. He sped the shortest way through the whole of Kadis and home to his sty behind Könik's and Eira's house. There he had been reared to the pig he was, and from there he would never again venture.

But Könik and Önde went back down to the river. Together they pushed the big boat out into the water, the boat that everyone in Kadis owned jointly. It had lain drawn up ever since that autumn when Jasper came home with the old doe rabbit. And the women came down to see what the men were doing. Bera had Jasper on her arm. Nikolavus was helpless in Borne's grip. He said not a word, he was as if in a trance, it was only natural and proper that they would kill him. And Eira said she would be glad to take care of that silver-threaded band that he had around his forehead. She would like to have a remembrance of him. ˙

228

Then Borne carried him to the boat and set him down on the stern thwart. That was where he had to sit and bail while they rowed him across the river.

When they got to the other side he had to climb out of the boat unaided. His legs were weak and he stumbled this way and that but nevertheless managed to get ashore. And Könik and Önde and Borne urged him on with terrible cries, they chased after him and drove him before them. He ran off as if he had completely lost his senses, and they shooed him away as they would a sheep or a goat or a rabbit. And so they forced him on until they were sure that he would never return, right into the forest proper, out into confusion and emptiness, down towards southern Sweden where he had come from.

When they rowed home again, Borne was the one who had to bail. A boat that has lain drawn up for a whole eternity has the most terrible leaks.


What else did they do that day?

Well, Borne showed Bera's teeth to everyone. And their wonder knew no bounds.

They grieved for Maria. Avar's and Ädla's Maria.

Könik planed a staff on which they would henceforth cut a notch for every day that passed. He would begin with the next day, and he would always carve the seventh diagonally across the one immediately before it.

And Eira helped him comb his hair over the ear that was missing. From that day on he always wore his hair like that.

Önde disappeared several times and dug a few holes on his own and buried things. Then he smoothed everything over afterwards so that nothing would show.

And Könik was examined and scrutinized. They almost didn't recognize him. By now no one could remember when his face had last been one coherent whole.

They also sat under Avar's rowan tree and talked about everything that now had to be done as a matter of absolute necessity. It was an unbelievable amount. But it would be achieved.

That wall that they'd always been talking about – now it would finally be built.

They said nothing about the rabbits. With the possible exception of what Önde muttered when chewing a little piece of dried meat. "It's white and sort of sweet, this is," he said, "and it soon fills you up. If only I could remember what kind of meat it is."

And when the time came, they would have to slaughter Blasius together, and they would have to divide him up among themselves. Such an absurd amount of meat and flesh. And Eira was so small even in the amount of food she ate.

And finally they lay down and slept in the light of the summer night, Borne with Bera and Könik with Eira and Önde by the far wall in Avar's house. His cow, who now might be any age at all, stood chewing the cud between him and Ädla. And there had not been such comforting sleep in Kadis since time immemorial. When they tried to remember when they had last slept such a sleep as this, their thoughts sank down into an abyss that seemed to them without end.

And the next day, in the morning, when they had eaten their porridge, Könik said: "Today is John the Baptist's Day." And he cut the first notch in the staff. But he said to Eira: "Help me remember that it's in the mornings that I count the time. If I ever once cut the staff in the evening, then all is lost."

Two strangers arrived in Kadis that day – indeed, not just two but perhaps even three. John the Baptist's Day, that is.

The first to come was the priest. His hair was fair and light and he was as big as Borne, and his teeth were broad and white and slightly protruding so that his upper lip slid up towards his gum as he spoke. He said his name straight away and no one had to tell him that this was Kadis. It was to Kadis that he'd been sent. He wanted to take possession of the chapel at once, no time was to be lost. They must celebrate Mass together for the first time that very day. He recognized the devil immediately when he saw him, Könik's old devil: he was to be put in the darkest corner of the chapel, almost invisible and discreetly unobtrusive, in keeping with his nature. It was also a matter of necessity that lots of other figures should be carved and set up in more prominent places: angels and saints and lambs and doves and virgins and prophets. Yes, Könik should certainly put his remarkable talents to work.

And they told him that there were only seven of them in all.

But that didn't bother him. "That's the way it is with people," he said. "Sometimes they're almost wiped out and sometimes there are such multitudes of them that they're like mosquitoes in a haystack. It's nothing to worry about: no more than one person at a time can appear before God, anyway." And he rubbed his hands and smiled at them. He felt like a farmer who was just about to start sowing in his newest field, he said. The little boy, Jasper, should be baptized, blessings must be administered, a marriage or two should be conducted, confessions must be heard, the dead should be committed to the earth in accordance with all the accepted rituals. Yes, he could see before him a field that he would plough and tend until the Day of Judgement. When he thought about his immense task in Kadis, this mission that could only be concluded in Eternity, he was filled with an almost paralyzing wonder and strength. And they would get a bell cast in Umeå, a bell that could be hung on a high scaffold frame like the one they had just made from new timber. He would ring it when they needed reminding of the proper division of time into hours, and of God, and above all of the order that cannot be seen but that resounds throughout the whole of existence with a peal that is audible and common to us all.

Yes. That was only right and proper. It was natural and self-evident. Now that he said it.

They gave him dried meat to eat and Bera fetched a goat's cheese and a can of goat's milk, and he praised the meat that was so light and tender and tasty even though it was so well dried that it would keep till Eternity.

The woman, he said with a smile, who had dried that meat, he would have liked to have had that woman, in his priestly way, as his own. He needed someone who would look after him and who understood dried flesh, a flesh where everything – yes, everything – had had to dry up and life's juices could only be experienced as taste and smell, refined and transformed.

"I'm the one who dried the meat," said Ädla. "And yes, I dare say I could be your woman."

*

232

At midday, just when the sun was at its highest in the sky, and everyone had gone to their own place to eat their midday soup, and the priest was eating with Ådla, and Önde had taken his cow and gone back home, a woman arrived. She came the same way that all strangers used to come, and she didn't go to Bera's house because Borne had closed the door so that Jasper could get his midday sleep without hearing the noise of the goats. So it was to Könik and Eira that she went. They were sitting eating on the threshold, both with their soup bowls in their hands. The woman was leading a very small boy by the hand; he was almost as big as Eira. In her other hand she had a large stout wicker basket.

Könik and Eira put down their soup bowls.

"I'll get you some soup," said Eira.

Könik moved over so that they could sit down.

"You get hungry and thirsty from walking," said the woman. "And I've had to carry this little one for long stretches."

"Yes," said Könik. "This sunshine is a blessing – but it saps your strength."

So they sat for a while talking about the weather and the world and distances.

Eira came back a few moments later with two bowls, a large one and a small one. She handed the large bowl to the woman, and she blew for a moment on the soup in the little bowl before she gave it to the boy.

"Now you shall eat, Kare," Eira said. "So that you get big and strong and wise like your father, Könik."

And the little boy had already learned how to open his mouth and form words.

"I haven't eaten soup," he said, "since Nordingrå."

"How do you know he's called Kare?" the woman asked.

"He's mine," said Eira. "I bore him myself and gave him that name."

For so it was. It was fitting and proper that it should be Kare. She didn't even need to look at the birthmark.

233

And Eira was quite simply so dizzy with happiness that she wouldn't have been able to help giving him the soup.

Könik lifted up the figure that he had hanging from a leather thong around his neck, the wooden figure that he'd carved when he was sitting in the lock-up. He inspected the boy and the figure, his eyes went between the image and the living face just as they used to in the old days between his models and the wood he was working on, and he saw that the likeness was complete. And he didn't allow himself even the slightest moment of thought or hesitation or doubt, he burst immediately into uncontrollable tears, he wept so much that his smooth face, which now had not even the shadow of a furrow, became completely shiny, and the tears that collected in his beard began to glitter like precious stones in the light.

And Kare ate the soup. He ate slowly and well. Eira, who had always known this moment would come, and Könik, who had never been able to imagine it, both sat there now in silence and watched him eating. Neither of them could even bear to blink.

When he'd finished, Kare licked the bowl absolutely clean.

And the woman told them how it all came about. It was terribly simple, it couldn't have happened in any other way.

She talked for a long time. Though the story itself was fairly short.

An unmarried man in Nordingrå had bought the boy in Hörnefors. He had paid a piece of cloth for him. And the seller had said that the boy was from up-country and was called Kare. But now the man had died. And she had some business in Kadis in any case, so she had brought him with her. There wasn't much more than Kadis up-country anyway. Yes, that's about how things were. The man had wanted a child of his own. And a piece of cloth, that was an uncommonly good price.

But Eira and Könik said nothing.

"Well, the thing was," the woman repeated, "I had some business here anyway."

"If you have business here," said Könik, "you'd better go to Önde."

"Who is Önde?"

She got no answer to that question. It was as if Eira and Könik didn't understand it. But Könik eventually dried his face and stood up and went out to the broad path that led to the houses further up. And he described the way to her and told her how she would recognize the house.

It was not until she had gone so far that she was no longer visible behind the corners of the houses that Eira and Könik remembered that they hadn't thanked her for giving Kare back to them. And they shouted after her simultaneously but she probably didn't hear it. They shouted at the tops of their voices: "Our thanks to you for Kare!"

They sat for a long time in the strange light just gazing at Kare. At last the soup and warmth made him sleepy and his head began to nod. Then Könik took him in his arms and carried him to the sty so that he could see Blasius. Könik wanted Kare too to be filled with a fitting sense of wonder.


And the woman went to Önde. He was sitting on his step and looking at the lilac tree that his wife Cecilia had planted. It was in bloom. The blossom was blue.

"Are you Önde?" she asked.

"Yes," said Önde.

"So I've come to the right place," the woman said, and put her wicker basket down on the grass.

"Yes," said Önde. "You might well have done."

"They told me that people with business here in Kadis should come to you."

"Yes," said Önde. "That's right."

And he lowered his head slightly and shifted his gaze from the lilac blossom to the woman. Her eyes were close-set and her nose was narrow and high-bridged. She had a birthmark on

235

her right cheek and a strange little gap between her front teeth. She was slightly knock-kneed.

She was pretty.

"My name is Maria," she said.

"Yes," said Önde.

Then she told him the business she'd come on.

There was once a man from Kadis who had come to Nordingrå. He'd never said what his name was, but he'd asked for her. He'd mentioned her name and described her accurately, he'd even known about the gap between her front teeth.

She pointed to the little gap with her middle finger.

And he'd said that she and no one else was the woman for him.

"Yes," said Önde.

But she'd been watching over the cows at Ulvön at the time and not heard anything about it until long afterwards.

"Well, yes," said Önde. "Yes, it was about that time of year."

She'd never been able to forget that man who'd trudged and tramped all the way from Kadis to Nordingrå for her sake. And now she'd walked the same path herself, but in the other direction. She'd had to do it before it was altogether too late. She couldn't live without meeting him, the man who was so certain he knew that she belonged to him. So now she wanted to ask Önde if he knew who this exceptional man might be.

"Yes," he said. "It was me."

For some moments they were both quite speechless.

She tried to scrutinize him carefully. She'd thought about him so very much that she felt she almost ought to recognize him. But it was hard because she had tears in her eyes.

Finally she had to run to him and bury herself in his arms, and he gripped hold of her and hugged her so tightly that Eira's soup came up into her mouth and for several moments she couldn't breathe. But after a while he lifted her up and carried her into the house and closed the door after them.

They were indoors for a long time. It was just him and her,

and of course the cow. They stayed there till the sun was no more than a foot or so above Scree Hill.

Then they came out and sat on the step. They had their arms round each other. They looked at the lilac tree.

But then Önde suddenly remembered something he'd begun to wonder about as soon as he saw her.

"What's that you've got in that wicker basket?" he asked.

And she had to fetch the basket and take out the peg and undo the clasp and lift the lid. Then she put both hands in and brought out a huge doe rabbit. She was black but with white tips on her ears. Önde couldn't remember ever having seen such an animal.

"Well, well," said Önde.

"It was a hare that made her pregnant," she said. "She must have twelve young'uns in her. As sure as I'm standing here."

And then Önde couldn't help but lift her up – yes, both her and the rabbit – and he carried her straight back into the house and immediately made love to her once more.